I0761001

TOM SHARP: THE MAN AND THE LEGEND

(A Novel)

CHARLIE STEEL
Tale-Weaver Extraordinaire

ILLUSTRATED BY
BARABASH SVIATOSLAV

TOM SHARP: THE MAN AND THE LEGEND

(A Novel)

CHARLIE STEEL
Tale-Weaver Extraordinaire

ILLUSTRATED BY
BARABASH SVIATOSLAV

CONDOR PUBLISHING, INC.
Lincoln, Michigan

TOM SHARP: THE MAN AND THE LEGEND (A Novel)

by Charlie Steel

August 2023

Library of Congress Control Number: 2023939904

ISBN-13: 978-1-931079-62-4

Condor Publishing, Inc.
PO Box 39
123 S. Barlow Road
Lincoln, MI 48742
www. condorpublishinginc. com

Printed in the United States of America

This book is dedicated to William Thomas Sharp

May 30, 1838 – November 26, 1929

Tom Sharp

"This is the West, sir. When the legend becomes fact, print the legend."
from The Man Who Shot Liberty Valance
(Director John Ford)

HISTORICAL CLARIFICATION AND DISCLAIMER

Although, Historical Fiction, this novel follows major events in this notable westerner's life. Tom Sharp was a remarkable character. He profoundly impacted the lives he encountered, and his positive contributions speak for themselves in advancing the settlement of the WEST.

Starting in 1868, Tom Sharp greatly affected the isolated area known as the Upper Huerfano River Valley, Colorado. This is specifically in the now nearly abandoned towns of Malachite and Gardner. It is located at the beginning of the Sangre de Cristo Mountains.

Much of the information in this novel is based on actual events and adventures that Tom Sharp experienced. However, the author embellishes and adds situations to honor Sharp's accomplishments.

He lived to 91 and died November 26, 1929, at the Buzzard Roost Trading Post location. The

Indian Chief Ouray and his wife Chipeta were real persons, as were Pueblo Priest Father Raverdy, Tex, John Miller, John White, John Williams, and Captain Deus. They all interacted with Tom Sharp during his lifetime. Character development is fictional but comes from the extrapolation of historical research.

As for Raine and other fictitious individuals interacting with Tom Sharp—it was the author's intent to develop well-rounded characters that dispel the myths and stereotypes surrounding Indians.

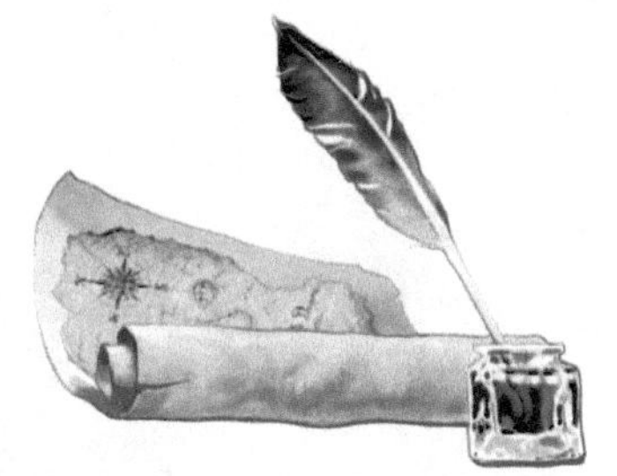

CHAPTER 1

General Sterling Price of the Army of the Confederate States of America entered the surgeon's tent. Soldiers lay on cots, others on the ground, their bandages soaked a bright crimson. Many of the men pleaded for help, young faces in pain, a few calling out to their mothers.

"Doctor, where can I find Private Tom Sharp?" asked the general.

"Don't bother me, man!" replied the doctor, bone saw in hand, his apron and arms soaked in blood.

The patient on the table began screaming. Price moved past the doctor as blood began to squirt. He looked for someone else to question. Stopping an aproned medical assistant, he asked the same question.

"General," responded the soldier, holding a full bucket of water, "Sir, sorry, sir, no one knows the names of these wounded men. If he's in here, you'll have to search…"

"All right, young man. Proceed with what you're doing."

Even for the general, the screams, the groans, the sights, and the sounds of so many wounded men were hard to take. Moving quickly now, searching the faces of young men, he went through the surgeon's tent and out the back, past a pile of human limbs. Turning away, General Price nearly ran to his tent.

Shouting to his adjutant as he entered the shelter, he gave explicit orders.

"Find Private Tom Sharp. He's somewhere among the wounded. When you locate him, get my surgeon to work on his wounds. Here, I'll put it in writing. Once that's done, give me a report on his condition."

"Yes, sir!" responded the young lieutenant picking up the hastily scribbled order.

General Sterling Price opened a wooden locker and pulled out a glass and bottle of whiskey. Hurriedly, he poured himself three fingers and emptied the glass. The images of gore and screams of the wounded soldiers were permanently embedded in his consciousness for the remainder of his life.

"How I hate this damn war," murmured the general.

The commander of Confederate troops continued to drink. The bottle was nearly finished before unconsciousness came to him.

"General! General!" shouted his lieutenant adjutant. "Sir, Tom Sharp was found."

Price opened his eyes and sat up.

"Well?"

"Sir, the doctor was none too pleased with the orders, but he stopped surgery to dress private Sharp's wounds. He says he is now a noncombatant. His injuries are serious and will take a long time to heal."

"Where is Sharp now?"

"Sir, he was carried to his tent and resting."

"Pour me some coffee, lieutenant, and bring me something to eat. When I'm finished, take me to him."

"Yes, sir!"

Cut-up chicken, corn, and a peeled and sliced apple filled the general's plate, served with a full pot of coffee. The java he drank in copious amounts, and only a small portion of the food was eaten. Rising, groggy, and hung over, the commanding officer relieved himself in a container. It would not be proper for the troops to see their general performing bodily functions.

"Adjutant, take me to Private Sharp!"

The lieutenant opened the tent flap, and fresh air blew away the smell of chicken and urine. General Price followed his man. Tom Sharp lay in a small soldier's tent, his body filling the space. The tent was opened and raised on one side. The adjutant brought a folding camp chair. The general waved the lieutenant and other soldiers away and sat down. He spoke just above a whisper.

"Glad to see you still breathing, Private," said the general.

"You will excuse me, sir. I can't salute or sit up. I…"

"That's all right, soldier. You're hurt; no formality here."

"Sir?"

"How are your wounds, lad?"

"Sir, the doc didn't take my leg, and I'm grateful, but it hurts something awful. The right arm hurts a

Chapter 1

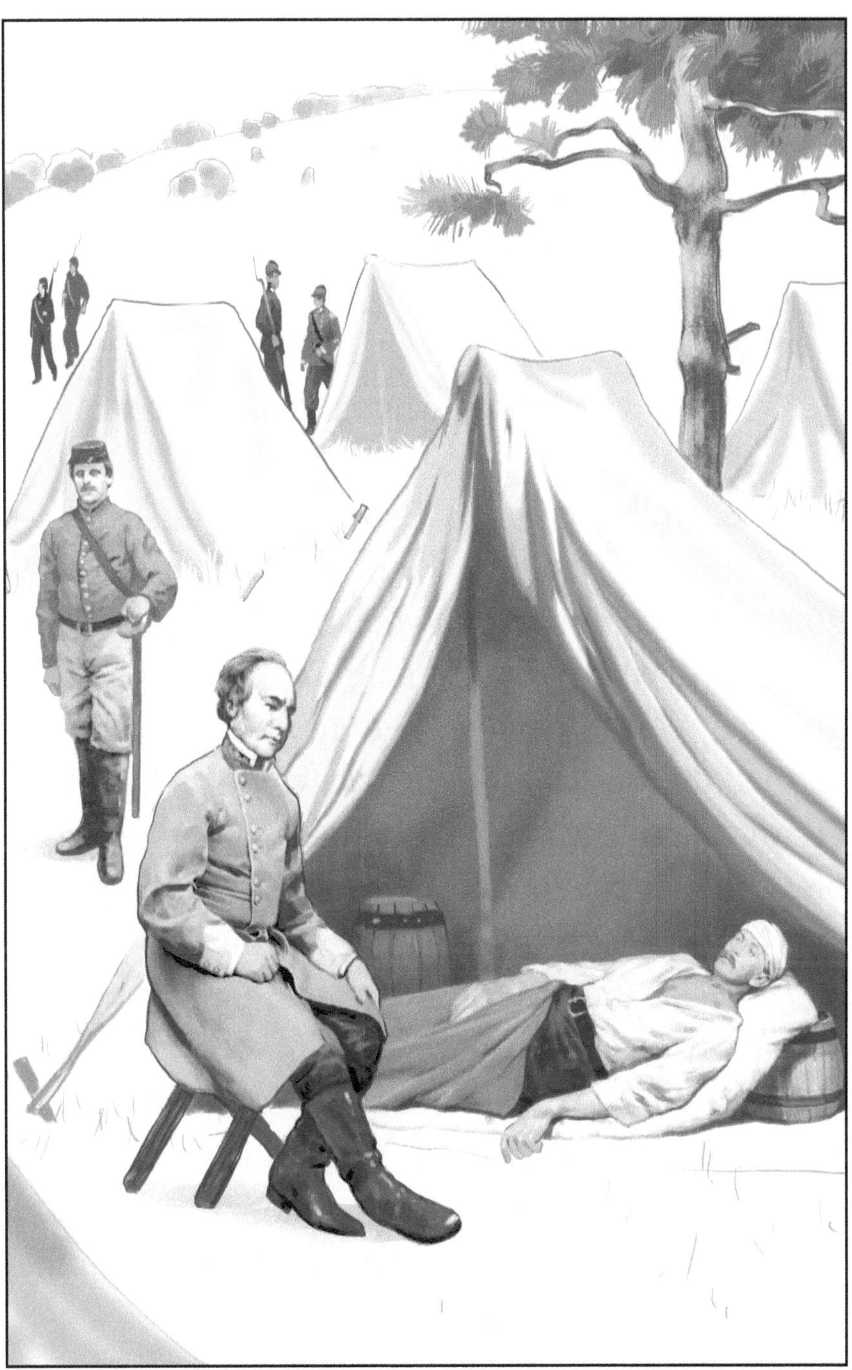

bit, and the bullet in my side just grazed me, but it…"

"Good. The pain is letting you know you're still alive. The doc that worked on you was my personal physician. We can't have a soldier like you just left to any sawbones."

"Sir?"

"You're wondering why a general comes to speak to a private?"

"Yes, sir."

"I've been watching you, Sharp. Fact is, I was going to promote you when you got wounded. Yesterday, when your captain and then the NCOs dropped, you ran and picked up the company flag and led the troops forward. I saw you in my glass. Despite taking three hits, you kept on. I reward brave men in my unit. The one thing I look forward to is coming here and speaking to you man to man.

"But, sir, they say I will be laid up a long time before my wounds heal."

"I know that from the doctor. I came here to ask where you want to be sent. Your enlistment will be over by the time you get well. I have in my hand a paper that discharges you. Good brave men in this war should get their rewards."

"Sir, I wasn't paid the last few months. I would like to go west, but I'm afraid Confederate money outside the South wouldn't…"

"West, you say?"

"Yes, sir."

"Don't you want to go home and be cared for?"

"I have been thinking about going west since I was a boy. When the war was declared, I joined. Even less reason to go home now. Sir, I want to make something of myself, and I don't think after the war, the South..."

"No politics, son. We'll leave that to our betters. We take orders, and they give them."

"Yes, sir. No offense, sir."

"None taken. You saved the battle yesterday, Sharp. Men were turning back until you picked up the colors. You did me a favor; I'll do you one. I know a group of southern families heading west away from the war. I'll purchase passage for you. Here's a $20.00 gold piece in reward. And I'll make sure your eleven dollars a month is paid in silver."

"Thank you, sir," said Tom Sharp. "I don't know what else to say."

"I'm thanking you. The wagon train leaves in a couple weeks. I figure you'll be well enough to lie in the back of a wagon by then. Until that time, recover here, and I'll make certain those southerners come to pick you up."

"Very kind of you, General."

"I won't ever admit I said this, son, but I wish I was going with you."

CHAPTER 2

Before his enlistment Tom Sharp made a marriage pact with the Durrett family. Mr. and Mrs. Durrett took a liking to the young man before he went off to war. They had allowed their seventeen-year-old daughter, Katherine, to accept an offer of betrothal. It was agreed that when Sharp made his fortune, he would return and marry her. Katherine, youthful and full of admiration for the young soldier, in truth, barely knew the man she agreed to wed.

It was, in fact, an arranged marriage. To keep the contract, the young man must write not to the daughter but to the parents. Sharp was now keeping his promise. In his very first letter, he wrote as a wounded soldier. He informed them of his release from duty by General Sterling Price and his pending travel west to seek his fortune. In his favor, he told them what the general said about him. He finished the letter and mailed it.

The wagon train picked up Tom Sharp, but it was not as he imagined. Ten wagons of hard and poor settlers were heading west out of desperation. Though the young man was quite ill from his wounds, the travelers didn't coddle the new addition. Breakfast was meager, and if Sharp wanted some of the bread and cheese, along with the cooked game, he had to climb off the wagon himself. The first day he fell, and it opened a hole in his leg. He began to bleed. No one came to help him. The group just stared, vacant-eyed and defeated. He managed to bind his wound and, with difficulty, got to his feet. He limped to the campfire, sat on a box, and took the plate that was handed to him.

"You plan on ridin' in that wagon all day?" asked the widowed father of a family of two boys and a little girl.

"I do," replied Sharp. "Until I'm able to walk normal."

"Well, do it quick, mister. The general paid me, but I didn't agree to no slackers. You do your fair share of work along the trail or find yourself left behind."

"I'm no slacker, Mr. Willoughby," said Sharp. "Never have been. But I'm miserable shot up, and you can't ask a man to do more than his wounds will let him."

"You mind your manners, and like I said, do your work, and we'll get along. A few more days, and I won't be letting you use those wounds as an excuse."

"You were paid, Willoughby, by the general himself. And I got this Yankee .36 Navy Colt, and you aren't cheating me nor the general, or I won't be the only one caring for a wound."

Willoughby spat and then laughed.

"I like a feller with spunk. But as I said, no slacking."

It was like that all along the trail. The wounds did get better, but it would be three weeks before Tom could perform simple work like gathering firewood and unhitching the mules. The children were sullen and didn't speak. Their father beat them if they so much as looked at him the wrong way. The rest of the wagon train wasn't much better. They were a sad, demoralized lot of folk.

The wagons moved slowly west, and Sharp's health further improved. He took it upon himself to become more useful by borrowing a horse from one of the more amenable wagoneers and went after game. With the first number of deer shot and the best proportions of meat brought back in their hides, the southern groups' disposition towards Tom Sharp changed. This was fresh meat they otherwise would not have. Tom was good with his .52 Sharps breechloader. It was an accurate weapon he confiscated off a dead Union officer. He was good with it, and it appealed to him that it carried his name.

It was evening, and the ten wagons formed their circle. They set up camp, unhitched, watered, and fed their stock. Earlier in the day, Sharp had ridden in with three bundles of choice deer meat, and he distributed it evenly among the wagons. Now the campfires were lit, and the smell of cooking venison permeated the air. People were relaxed, and some even smiled in anticipation of the welcome repast.

"You think you're big stuff now's you bringin' in game," complained Willoughby to Sharp.

The daughter of the surly man was cooking. The man's two sons sat on a big rock near the fire, drinking from tin cups and waiting for supper.

"I don't see you favorin' us," continued Willoughby. "How's come you be givin' the loin and best pieces to others?"

"I mete out the venison in fair proportions," said Sharp. "Sorry you don't see it that way."

"I don't. We gives you a ride in our wagon, and now's you feelin' good, you work for others."

"Nobody is favored," said Sharp. "I saw a need, and borrowing a horse, I was able to fill it. I will keep on doing so until we reach our destination."

"Sharp," said Willoughby, "I don't like you, never have. Pretending to be ill and lazin' around in my wagon, and then you rear up on your hind legs and show off to all these folks. I don't want you around here."

"You were paid to take me west by General Sterling Price. In his good name, you'll keep your word."

"Or what?" shouted the surly southerner.

Tom Sharp took off his shirt and revealed lean muscle. Willoughby removed his. The big man was a head taller than Sharp and had fifty pounds or more over him in weight. The disagreeable fellow had a paunch; Sharp appeared wiry and slim. The entire wagon train left their cookfires and gathered to watch the confrontation.

"I've had my fill of fighting," said Sharp. "But I see you're not an honorable man, in word or deed. For a long time now, I've seen you beat your children and without good cause. We've all stood by and did nothing. You are a disgusting, loud-mouthed bully. If you think you can pound on me without retribution, have at it."

"Fancy words," replied Willoughby in a taunting voice.

"Unlike you, my family believes in books and education."

"Are you calling me stupid?"

"If the word fits," replied Sharp.

In the sudden silence, the combined gasping sound from the seasoned travelers was loud.

"You pot-licker!" shouted Willoughby. "I'm gonna stomp you in the ground!"

The big man stepped forward and close to Sharp, his huge hands clenched into fists. He raised his arms and threw a right roundhouse punch. Tom Sharp ducked and put a right into Willoughby's belly. The man gushed air and bent over, and when he did, Sharp kicked his right foot into the aggressor's shin. The bully stood erect and howled in pain. Sharp struck quickly with fists, a left and right to either side of the mouth, and then a terrific uppercut to the chin. Willoughby closed his eyes, teetered, and out cold, fell backwards onto the ground with a terrific thud. Dust rose, and the nasty southerner did not move. The crowd roared, clapped, and whistled in enthusiastic support.

"Serves him right!" shouted a man.

"The big bully!" said a woman.

"About time he got what he deserved," exclaimed another.

The fight over, the group of weary travelers returned to their campfires and their dinner of fresh venison.

CHAPTER 3

The wagon train followed others along the Oregon/California Trail. The grass was frequently eaten, and they had to move further away at night to find forage for the animals. Game, too, was scarce from those who came before. Tom Sharp could not always find fresh meat.

After months of struggling forward, the group became even more weary and sullen. Willoughby was the worst of the bunch, but thanks to Sharp, the rest of the pioneers now stood up to the man and didn't allow him to beat his children.

Foraging away from the wagon train, Sharp was glad to be out on his own. All along the Nebraska Territory the buffalo herds were enormous. Taking a pack horse, the ex-Confederate soldier killed a small bull, butchered it, and packed away a hundred pounds of choice meat. He prepared two large bundles wrapped in canvas and tied them to his horse.

Then a voice startled Sharp.

"Say, feller, if I had the inclination, you'd be dead."

Sharp jerked around, a pepperbox pistol in his hand. He stared at a man wearing buckskins and a leather band wrapped around his head. Whoever he was, his face was burned brown by the sun and showed age and deep wrinkles. He looked like a native of the West, hard and experienced. And the weapons he carried showed he was no one to fool with.

"Where did you come from?"

"Been watching you for the last hour. Ever since you fired that Sharps and dropped that buff. A feller out here needs to look up real keerful like and scout once in a while. This here's flat land; you didn't look up but twice."

"Who are you, mister?"

"Ain't no mister. Indians call me one thing, and whites another. I prefer Tex."

"My name's Sharp, Tom Sharp. Do you want some of this meat? There's still plenty left."

Sharp slid the pepperbox back into a pocket.

"I'll pass. You have the same name as that rifle you're carryin'. You related?"

"Huh, I wish."

"What you doin' out here by yourself?"

"I'm with a wagon train," replied Sharp. "Gathering meat for…"

"I spotted a party of Lakota Sioux north of here. They're off their summer camp. It might be trouble if they catch you out here alone. If I heard that shot, they did too."

"I'm going," said Sharp. "You wanna come with me?"

"I don't know you, and you don't know me," said Tex.

"No, but if you were to cause me trouble, you could have and didn't. Besides, I've got an interest in this country. Especially on how to earn money from it."

"What ya have in mind?" asked Tex.

"I need to learn how to survive out here. I can't do it by myself. Suppose we get to know each other and talk about it."

Tex laughed.

"Sounds to me like you're sick of those folk on the wagon train."

"That might be part of it," said Sharp, smiling. "And I don't have a friend in the world out here or a way of making money. At least not yet."

"Well, I did see you take a mighty fine shot on that buff. And you ain't afraid of blood or to git your hands dirty. That's a plus."

By the time Tex and Sharp made their way to the wagon train, both men had enough time to size each other up. At least enough to make a decision to head west together.

Tex and Sharp rode in. It was evening, and the wagons were circled for the night. In the light of a campfire, together, they helped unpack the buffalo meat to distribute. Sharp went to the owner of the horse and tack he was borrowing and asked to buy it. It took some palavering, the price going at thirty dollars, nearly all of Sharp's money. The silver and the twenty-dollar gold piece the general gave him helped cinch the deal. Taking advantage of the crowd, Sharp stepped forward.

"Folks, this here fellow is named Tex. He's been living on the plains and in the mountains most his life. I made a deal with him: we're to partner up and head west, hunting and selling meat. I'll be leaving in the morning, but before I go, I want to thank you for your hospitality."

"I wouldn't have sold you the horse if I had known that," commented the previous owner.

"Who's going to bring in fresh meat for us?" asked another, and the crowd murmured assent.

"I'm sorry, folks," said Sharp. "Maybe Willoughby could take over that task for you."

"Good riddance," said the mean southerner. "Hope you get scalped."

The crowd hissed at the comment.

"We hate to see you go," said one of the men, and the wagon members called out similar comments.

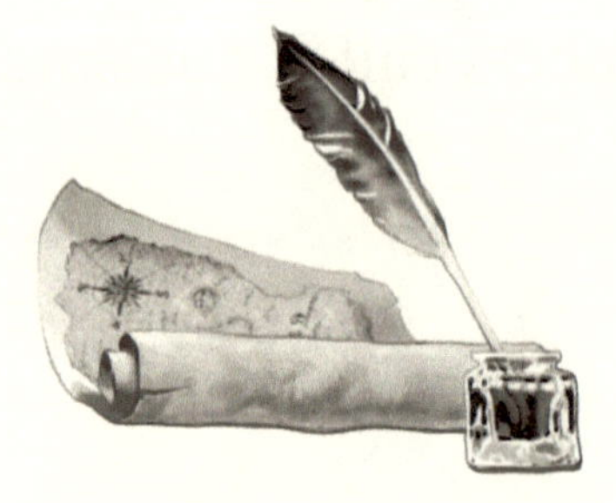

CHAPTER 4

Tex kicked the bottom of Tom Sharp's feet, hanging out from under Willoughby's wagon. It was still pitch black.

"Pack up your bedroll, and let's mosey on out of here. Hate crowds and goodbyes."

Sharp did as he was told, upended, thumped the heels of his boots against unknown critters, then stomped into them and buckled on his Navy Colt. There was little to pack: a canteen, the pepperbox pistol, his Sharps carbine, a few items of clothing, canvas, and a ragged blanket bedroll. Stepping outside the circle of wagons, Tex came forward with his partner's saddled horse.

"Let's ride. By dawn, we ought to be ten miles from these folks. Good riddance. Can't stand greenhorns."

"I'm one," replied Sharp.

"Yeah, but I got plans for you. A feller that survives three wounds in that there war ought to be able to handle the trail. You pick up on what I show you, and we'll git along."

They rode all morning without further conversation, the newcomer following the native westerner. Instead of riding out in the open, Tex found cover from trees and vegetation, and when that wasn't possible, lowland that hid their presence as they headed west. Eventually, they reached a large water hole enveloped with thick cottonwood trees. They dismounted and pulled the bits from their horses mouths and allowed them to drink and graze.

"What did you learn so far, partner?" asked Tex.

"You kept to cover, low ground, and didn't expose yourself or your horse."

"Like I thought, you ain't stupid. Pay attention. You never know what you'll encounter out here. Indians hereabouts hate whites and are just plum unfriendly. Then there's them soldiers from both sides of the war, come robbin' and killin'. And those wagons bring along all kinds of peculiar fellers. That doesn't count the miners, pioneers, active soldiers, immigrants and their funny tongues, and some crazies. This West is filling up with all kinds. That's a fact, and I warn you not to trust a one of 'em."

"That's a lot to take in," replied Sharp. "So far, I trust you."

"Yeah, that's something else I wanted to say. You was far too trustin' with me. Don't never do it again, you hear? You got lucky two ways."

"How's that?"

"That I didn't slit your throat and that I was lookin' for a partner."

"Then why me?"

"I liked your color," laughed Tex. "Now's we's in both worlds. The further West we go, the more you need me. I's got one foot in the Indian world, and you got two feet in the white. Together, we both have a chance to survive out here."

"Never thought of it that way. You know a lot about me, but I hardly know anything about you."

"That's another thing to learn. The Indian way is not to reveal too much about yourself. That way, you keep your power. Sharp, you need to think on that. Be keerful what you say."

"Keep your power? That is something to ponder. Are you going to tell me anything?"

"Like what?" asked Tex.

"Like what Indian tribe you're…"

"My father was a mountain man, respected by the Arapaho. He took an Indian wife, and that was my ma."

"Thank you for that. And you speak..."

"I speak Arapaho, Spanish, and bits and pieces of others. More important, I know sign. Out here, all the tribes know it. I'll be teachin' you that along the way."

"Thanks."

"This is the most I spoke in five years. Now let me catch a couple panfish, and we'll fix a quick fire, eat, and git out of here. Another thing, critters and people come to water. Out here, best to camp away from water holes and to keep your fire hidden and brief. Smoke and smell travel a long way too."

Cooked panfish on a stick didn't taste bad with salt. Refreshed, the men rode the rest of the day and into the dark. They made camp in a thicket of cottonwoods, scaring out a big bear. Unsaddling and hobbling the horses on a patch of grass, they started a small fire to boil coffee and ate jerky. Laying out their bedrolls, Tex walked around checking for snakes, put out the fire, and then lay down for the night.

They woke in the morning, each man turned and slapped his boots. A small copperhead slithered out of one of Tom Sharp's. Using a stick, he flipped it into the brush. Tex laughed.

"Partner, don't know how many steps you would've taken, but it would have made you sick for quite a spell."

"I don't see anything funny about it," said Sharp, tapping both boots for extra measure.

"Before this trip to Californy is over, there will be a lot more serious happenin' than that."

"You've decided?" asked Sharp.

"That's the best place to sell meat. Gold miners, hard rock mining, men with money in their pockets. You know a better place to gain coin?"

"But after all this time, will there be any game?"

"Partner," replied Tex, "I can track meat on the hoof over solid rock. Just see if we don't load up on mule deer and elk. Come on, pack up; daylight's coming."

They traveled through the vast open areas of the unending Nebraska Territory. The land stretched far ahead, flat as a pancake. Tex pushed hard, and each day they covered nearly forty to fifty miles, sometimes more. They were traveling three times faster than a wagon train, and they avoided the ones they came upon.

The first group of Indians they encountered was Arapaho. Tex rode straight up to them. The half-breed said something, and the twelve warriors laughed. The language sounded strange with unusual articulation. Tom Sharp did as he was told and stayed well back. After some talk, Tex signaled for Sharp to ride forward.

“They invited us to their camp,” whispered Tex. “Don’t talk, don’t do nothin’ but what I tell you. They ain’t feelin’ too kindly to whites. I’ll explain tonight.”

They rode into the village behind the warriors. Two boys took their horses, and the guests were led to the largest tipi. The structures were arranged mainly in a circle with their opening flap to the east. The two visitors stood outside. There was much discussion between several young warriors, before Chief Nawat, known in English as Chief Long Hand, greeted them. Angry gestures were made against Tom Sharp, who did his best to stand and make little eye contact. Tex came to his friend.

“Say nothin’, do nothin’. Behind you is a campfire. Go sit on the log and stare at no one.

This may take some time. These people are angry at broken treaties, slaughtered game, and the immigrant wagons that keep coming. I will talk to the chief and try our best to leave with our hair."

Sharp did as told and sat at the fire. From the corners of his eyes, he saw the Indian women, warriors, and children give grimacing looks. In the war, there were times when he was afraid, and others, when disregarding his life, he ran forward into enemy fire. Here, it was worse; he could do nothing but trust his newfound friend.

After a long hour, Tex emerged from the chief's tipi and came forward.

"It's bad," said the frontiersman. "These people are mad about the treaty at Fort Wise ceding land to the government. They didn't sign it and once again felt tricked by the whites. Because of the war, there are few troops out here, and the Cheyenne, Sioux, and Arapaho are convinced that unless they fight, all land will be lost, and they will be forced onto reservations. They've got our horses and supplies. We'll have to wait and see if we can get out of this."

"But you are part Arapaho," said Sharp.

"Yeah," said Tex, "and the other part ain't. What's goin' for us is that we were brought in by members of the tribe. It ain't hospitable to kill a guest."

An elderly Indian came up to Tex and thumped him hard on the back. Tex whirled around and, when he saw who it was, shouted, "Thunder!" The two men hugged and smiled. They spoke for some time in their language then the Indian looked to Tom Sharp.

"You either foolish white man or brave idiot," said Thunder. "Either way, come to my tipi. Inside, we smoke, we talk, we eat, we sleep."

The next morning, Tex and Sharp were brought their horses, and they rode at a walk out of the village. Then for a mile, they turned to a trot and then to a dead run. They encountered a small herd of buffalo, and Tex galloped right through the middle, pushing the large animals before him for as long as he could to confuse their tracks. The horses became sweaty and lathered with foam. Tex finally slowed his to a walk, and Sharp came up beside him.

"You did good," said Tex. "You kept your mouth shut and your eyes straight ahead."

"So why are we running?"

"There are warriors in that camp that want our scalps. It will be touch and go for the next few days. One of those is an enemy of my youth. I'll be looking for low and hard ground. We ain't out of this yet."

"But Thunder was a friend of yours."

"He helped raise me. He saved us, Sharp. Someone up there is watching out for us."

"But I don't understand."

"Yes, you do. Soon as what you call the Great Conflict is over, this land is goin' to be crawling with even more immigrants and soldiers. Already they're shootin' buffs for hides and tongues and lettin' the rest rot. Ain't no better way to rile an Indian."

"What are you saying?"

"The ride to Californy for one white and a breed out on the trail alone ain't gonna be no pleasure trip. The tribes are riled. And no right-thinkin' man will have trouble understandin' the reason. Their land is bein' stolen. There's gonna be war, and that kinda fightin' for the tribes will be murder on both sides. The Indians will get the worst of it. Like the buffalo, it'll be a wonder any of 'em survive."

Tex and Sharp rode in silence through the dark before stopping at a roiling spring. Dismounting, they watered the horses, removed bits, and let them graze. They filled canteens, ate jerky, and walked around getting relief from riding. Repast finished, they put foot to stirrup and traveled by star and moonlight. With caution, the men rode all night and into the morning before making camp. They found a rock formation and spread their bedrolls behind it.

At daylight, they awoke stiff and sore. The horses needed more attention and were rubbed down and taken out to graze. Foregoing breakfast, they saddled, mounted, and headed west. Looking for a better camp, Tex pointed towards a small lake. Riding through shallow water to hide tracks, they stopped at the far end in a grove of cottonwoods. Both horses and men were exhausted. The mounts were hobbled on grass among the trees. Sharp threw his bedroll on the ground, lay down, and instantly fell asleep.

Tex looked to his partner, smiled grimly, and shook his head. He took out hook and line and began fishing. He was rewarded with several panfish. Making a fire, he cleaned and cooked his catch. Waking Sharp with the toe of his boot, both men ate.

"I've never been so sore," said Sharp.

"Not even when wounded, three times?"

"Well…that's different. How many miles you think we rode?"

"Over a hundred, I reckon. We was hard on the horses. Hate to do it, but I figure we better hole up here a couple days. Not so much for us, but for them."

Since leaving the wagon train, this was the first time the men lazed around. They took turns fishing, catching panfish and chubs. Hungry, they ate all they caught and slept the rest of the day. The next morning, Tex kicked Tom Sharp awake.

"What?" asked Sharp, annoyed at his partner.

"If you was to be set out here on the prairie or up in the mountains without a hoss, weapon, matches, clothing, what would you do?"

"What's this about?" asked Sharp. "You woke me up from a sound sleep to ask me that?"

"You sleep too much, my friend. Today school starts. I be learnin' you some life lessons."

Tired of fish and out of coffee, the men drank water and chewed on jerky. Then Tex showed how to construct a fire bow from a leather string and a bent stick. It took a while, but Sharp was able to start several fires. Then they moved on to flint and steel. With that, Sharp got smoke but no fire.

"Pay attention; it's the tinder you use that makes the difference. This here could save your life. Since the beginnin', our people have been startin' fires this way."

After several hours and untold attempts, both men gave up.

"Why am I doing this?" asked Sharp.

"This afternoon, anytime, hostiles of all kinds could catch up with us. I could be kilt, your possessions taken, and say you survive. What then?"

"I don't know."

"Darn right, you don't. Now pay attention. See this here, milkweed? The pods, young stems, and leaves can be boiled and eaten. At certain times of year, there are wild nuts and berries. See this plant? It's called the yellow lotus and grows in marshy places. Peel the stems of the water lily or take the unrolled leaves and boil them to eat. Here's a cattail. They're not too hard to find. Pick and cook the tender white shoots. Doesn't taste bad at all. Are you paying attention, Sharp? I ain't speakin' just to hear myself talk."

"I'm listening," said Sharp.

"You better be. Cause when I'm done palavering and before the day is out, you're gonna pick all these things I'm talking about, cook, and eat 'em."

The blank stare on Sharp's face irritated Tex, and he stood straight up.

"Listen, partner, what I'm teachin' you, ain't no joke. Ah, the heck with it. Just let me tell you, I was taught this as a kid. There are turkey peas, wild potatoes, wild grapes, wild plums, and chokecherries to eat all over this country at the right time of year. Then if you're really hungry, there's lizards, snakes, grubs, and insects. If you want to live, you'll eat 'em, and they'll keep you alive."

"I'm not ignoring you. I'm just tired. Keep talking."

"You better be listening. Pick enough of those plants I showed you for the two of us. About time we had something green to eat. Use my little skillet. I'll catch more fish to go with 'em."

"All right, Tex. But we're out of salt and coffee, and I sure would like some airtights. I'm hankering for a can of peaches and beans, but I'm short of money."

"Over yonder is the Platte River. We've stayed away from it to avoid trouble. It looks like we lost those kin folk of mine a while back, or we'd be dead by now. Fort Laramie is a couple hard days' ride up ahead. I've got enough coin to buy supplies."

That afternoon it was Sharp who cooked. He boiled milkweed leaves, peeled water lily stems and young shoots of cattails, along with fish on a stick. The fish tasted bland without salt. The next morning they were up before dawn and broke camp. The horses kicked in complaint to be ridden after two full days and nights of rest. They rode until dark and made a cold camp. Again they had water and jerky. Sleeping the night through, they were up at daylight, hurrying to Fort Laramie and a good meal.

Before noon, Tex and Sharp crossed the North Platte River.

"Looky yonder, there's the fort," said Tex. "And beyond that, you can see the Laramie River. They got protection on both sides."

"Why are there tipis?" asked Sharp.

Cheyenne, Arapaho, Sioux, and other tribes were camped across the Laramie River.

"If the Indians are planning war, why are they…"

"Haven't you heard?" said Tex. "Keep your friends close and your enemies closer?"

"Still…"

"They're just like us. They trade for tobacco, food, and supplies."

They rode up to the fort, and the guards let them pass. There were impressive buildings inside the open area; it was a very large compound. Tom Sharp stared like a schoolboy at the two-story wooden barracks. The two men tied their horses at the sutler's store and went inside. They passed endless goods for sale. To the side was a sutler's bar for the enlisted. They sat down at a round table and ordered food and beer. The sutler gave the fish eye to the dark-skinned Tex. Both men ate like bears after a long winter. The bill came, and Tex cursed.

"The prices at these sutler stores are always crazy," he said. "Come, let's buy what we can and get out of here. I hate crowds. The less my people see of me or you, all the better."

"Why?"

"In less time than it took us to ride here, Chief Long Hand will know where we've been. Even from Nebraska, he could give orders for our scalps."

"I didn't think about that."

"The vast distances don't mean that anyone escapes notice."

"Sure," said Sharp. "And the telegraph will make it even more so."

They purchased tobacco, bags of salt, pepper, airtights, ammunition, dry beans, coffee, jerky, pots, a pan, utensils, tin plates and cups, a bridle, bit, and reins, trade knives, rope, and a double sided pannier to put everything in. Outside the fort, Tex rode up to a herd of Indian mustangs. He made sign for trade. A blanket was laid on the ground, and Sharp watched from a distance. A pot, two knives, a pouch of tobacco, and silver coins were slowly added before a Cheyenne warrior nodded his head.

Led by the Cheyenne, Tex went into the herd and examined teeth, hooves, and legs of several horses. He ran his hand down the coat of a paint he selected. The Cheyenne trader and Tex nodded their heads and signed. The horse his partner brought up to Sharp was extraordinary.

"I was going to use this one as a packhorse," said Tex, "but he's too good a critter not to ride. I'll change saddles and put a lead rope on my other hoss and tie down the panniers."

Tex did as he explained. But when he tried to put the saddle on the paint, it didn't want any part of it. It took both men to hold the reins and bend an ear before the saddle could be cinched. A group of Indians came closer. In front was the Cheyenne

Chapter 4

who made the trade. He was smiling. Tex put his foot to the left stirrup, and just as he got his right leg over, the paint began bucking. It made a vicious circle to the left and threw the rider to the ground. The horse turned, looked at the prone man, and whinnied. Indians grunted and clapped.

With determination and Sharp's help, they got the paint to settle down. This time Tex was ready. In an instant, he was on the saddle and both feet in the stirrups. The paint bucked, whirled, hopped, and ran forward, bucked and whirled again but could not dislodge its rider. Tex put spurs to the mustang. The horse snorted in fear and pain and leaped into a dead run. Faster than it seemed possible, horse and man ran straight for the Platte River and splashed across. The horse ran flat out for some distance before Tex could get it to turn and head back. Finally, the paint and the man, dripping wet, rode up to the group of Indians who were laughing, clapping, gesturing, and grunting comments in their own language.

"I didn't expect that," said Tex, grimacing in pain. "I'll have to tame this monster and use rope and hobbles before he knows who's master."

Tex, not daring to dismount, asked Sharp to take over the lead rope of the packhorse, and together, the two men and three horses crossed the Platte and headed west. The Indians were still gesturing and laughing at the unexpected entertainment.

"Those Cheyenne sure got a kick out of your riding."

"That devil." said Tex, "The horse trader knew all along this hoss was trouble. They were taking bets if I could stay on him. No doubt I lost that feller every trade good and coin I gave him."

"Indians gamble?" asked Sharp.

"You bet. Indians aren't different than whites when it comes to making a bet. Horse races most of all."

They rode all day in silence, no need to take a lunch, as they had such a big meal at the fort. That night they drank coffee and feasted on airtight beans and, for dessert, a can of syrupy peaches. Tired, they hobbled the horses, and true to his word, Tex put a rope on the paint and tied it to a tree.

Early in the morning, both men awoke to three scruffy scavengers standing over them, holding a musket, a pistol, and a shotgun.

"Looky here," said one of the bearded, brown-toothed thieves, "two sleeping beauties!"

"Hey, Red," said a second fellow, "look at these here panniers. They's full of all kinds of food and stuff!"

"Three horses, a Sharps, two Colts, and a Henry," said the third fellow. "Shoot 'em, Red, and let's have breakfast."

"Nawww, I want to play with them a bit. Look at them all snug in their bedrolls."

"Watch it now," said the second fellow, "no tellin' what's under them blankets."

"Burt," said Red, "you pull those covers off them fellas. Do it quick."

Burt did as he was told. Tom Sharp lay on canvas in white long johns and socks. Tex was fully dressed, his boots up by his head. Sharp looked to his partner and said nothing.

"I see no weapons," said Burt. "But we don't know these skunks. Shoot 'em, Red."

"Naw, I don't see no fear yet. Burt, you get the hosses. Frank, you pick up the treasures and fill those panniers."

"What are you gonna do with them fellas?" asked Frank.

"You no never mind," said Red, "do as I say."

"Red," said Burt, "we's be walking no more."

Burt went for the three horses. It took some time for him to saddle two of them, remove the hobbles, and bring the horses forward. The paint gave him the most trouble, but he managed to bring all three.

“Help me put the panniers on this paint.” said Frank.

“Do it yourself,” ordered Red.

Tex kept trying to catch Sharp’s eye, and when he did, he nodded his head and mouthed silent words. To Sharp, it looked like, “Watch me.”

When Frank tried to put the panniers on the paint, the horse reared back. Angry, Frank jerked viciously on the reins, and blood squirted from the animal’s jaw. The big horse moved forward and took the man’s arm in his mouth and bit down hard, and did not let go. Frank screamed and screamed as the horse backed up, head high, holding the man on his toes as he danced like a marionette.

Distracted, Red and Burt turned their eyes to their distressed partner. Tex reached into his boot, pulled out a knife, and came to his feet. He stepped forward and plunged it into Red’s heart. Tom Sharp grabbed a pepperbox pistol from under his saddle, the one he carried in the war. He jumped to his feet, and when Burt turned with his heavy musket, Sharp shot him in the face. Red and Burt now lay dead on the ground while the paint still held Frank’s arm and tossed him around like a rag doll. Then the big horse turned his body and whacked head and torso of the tormented man against a cottonwood tree.

Both Tex and Sharp heard the terrific impact. Frank fell dead in a twisted mess of blood and gore. And then the paint commenced repeatedly stomping on the dead body.

"Well," said Sharp, "I don't want to go through that again."

"You did well, partner," said Tex, "where'd you come up with that strange pistol?"

"Carried it in the war. Most of us did. It's small and gets the job done."

"That it does," said Tex. "Come on, let's pack up and get out of here."

"What about the bodies?"

"Let 'em lie where they're at. I can smell every one of 'em from here. Those three fellers are about the saddest lot I ever saw."

"You know we owe your horse our lives."

Tex laughed.

"We do. Wish I had some oats. But the next stop will be on good grass, and I'll personally pick it and hand-feed that monster. Sure hope I can make friends with him. Hate him to do that to me."

The two travelers finished dressing, gathered their weapons, and gingerly stepped over the dead. They put together their bedrolls, removed a saddle from the packhorse, and loaded the panniers. Tex, talking softly to the paint, managed to calm him down. It took time, but Sharp and Tex could eventually saddle the paint. With difficulty, Tex mounted his nervous mustang, and together the two men rode out of their gory camp. They rode west toward a long line of cottonwoods miles away. In the trees, they found another small lake and lush grass growing around it. Both men let the horses drink. Tying reins, true to his word, Tex picked an armful of grass, and taking it to the paint, he hand-fed the horse.

"Boy," said Tex, "you and me are gonna be friends."

While the big paint ate, the dark-skinned man carefully laid a hand along the neck of the horse. The mustang nickered, and Tex kept up the long gentle stroking.

The stop didn't take long. Both men were anxious to ride as far as they could from their morning altercation. And that is exactly what they did, riding until well past dark before picking out a camp.

Over a quick fire, they cooked and ate. Setting out their bedrolls, they lay down for sleep.

"I told you ya," said Tex, "there's all kinds of danger out here. But partner, that was a close call. I don't ever remember seein' such filthy beasts as those men."

"Tex, they were despicable creatures. I figure neither one of us will be forgetting."

Crickets chirped loudly around them, followed by the familiar calls of hunting coyotes. Then came the hoot of an owl. To these familiar night sounds, both men went to sleep. This time they were not careless, their weapons close at hand.

The next day, they traveled past dark and camped far off the Oregon/California Trail. In the coming weeks, they made fifty miles or more a day. They resupplied at Fort Bridger and hurried on, staying some distance from the main trail. Skirting around Salt Lake City, the two kept pushing hard for California. Living off the land, both men and animals became harder and leaner.

Ragged and dirty, they bathed when they could. They forgot the names of days or how many weeks it took to reach the Humboldt River. Resting a day, they crossed the Forty Mile Desert and reached the Truckee River. Following it to the foot of the Sierra Nevada Mountain range, they climbed up the pass.

"Mighty pretty country," said Sharp.

"Careful there, partner, but I might be inclined to take a bite out of you."

"You gone loco? What are you talking about?"

Tex laughed long and hard.

"Fella, you're standin' dead on Donner's Pass. There are two meanings there."

Tom Sharp looked around in wonder, mouth open. Everyone knew about the Donner Party. There wasn't a kid that hadn't made a remark about it in their childhood. Finally, Sharp thought up a response.

"I'm not dead, Tex, not yet. And, I guarantee you, partner, I wouldn't taste good. As a matter of fact, no one's ever going to carve on and chew my buttocks."

Both men laughed.

"I wouldn't be so certain on that," replied Tex. "After meetin' those three back there on the trail, anything's possible out here. And there's bears, and catamounts, and…"

"They don't count. We were talking of humans eating…"

"Tell that to the bear when he's chewin' on your rump," said Tex and guffawed.

This was the most the two had talked in weeks, and it was the first time they laughed since the ambush way back in Dakota Territory.

CHAPTER 5

All along the California Trail, they had done their best to ride hidden and away from other travelers. Now, heading for Sacramento, they were encountering miners and mule trains with supplies. Eventually, they came to wagon roads filled with teamsters carrying equipment to the hard rock mines.

"How are we going to carry meat and sell it?" asked Sharp.

"We'll need mules, salt, and customers," replied Tex. "If we can't get mules, we'll buy horses. If we can't buy them, we'll get burros. If we can't do that, we'll use the horses we have until we earn enough to get what we need."

"Sounds like hard work."

"The trip here was easy. Huntin' in the mountains, findin' herds of elk, shootin' them, cuttin', saltin' and packin' the meat, won't be no picnic."

"Wouldn't buying cattle from Californios or ranchers be easier?" asked Sharp. "We could get two wagons, and we would be able to carry more."

"Sounds like you've been thinkin' on this," replied Tex. "But it would depend on good trails."

"I'm certain the big mining companies have roads by now."

"I reckon. But still, we have no money, and we'll have to find customers and start out my way first. Then maybe yours later."

It took a lot of work to find game in gold mining country. But true to his word, Tex located herds of elk in the high mountains. It was torture climbing up and down the steep cliffs and chasing after the animals they downed. They salted the meat and sold it to mining companies, miners, and those that had families. Both men saved their coin. Their business gave them a profit, but the work was hard.

Buying wagons and selling beef was easier, but the competition was tough. Eventually, in 1863 they moved on to Oregon. They sold meat to gold miners at Blue Canyon and Freezeout creeks. This lasted until 1865. It was there Tom Sharp became restless.

"Tex," said Sharp one Sunday afternoon.

It was one of the rare times when they were not working.

"Yeah?"

"Tex, I have a hankering to do something else," said Sharp.

"I thought on it too, but can't think of anything. We've worked hard to get this far. Don't you like my company?"

"I like it fine, partner. But I need to earn more money and save up. There's a girl back in Marion County, Missouri. She'd be grown up by now. I know it's old-fashioned, but her parents sort of picked me out to be her husband. I can't go back broke."

"You ain't broke," said old Tex. "I'm older than you, and I know how far coin goes. The money in that belt around your waist will take you a long ways."

"Not far enough, Tex. I got ambition to have a ranch, raise cattle, breed horses, marry, and have children."

"Whoa, partner. You never said a word."

"Tex, you never say much yourself, and I know you don't like me blabbing. I think mainly that's why we got along."

"You're leaving, ain't you?"

"Yes. I don't want you riled at me, but I corresponded with a feller named John Miller. He says he's got a contract to cut and supply telegraph poles to the Union Pacific Railroad up in Dakota Territory. I am hankering to see the country, and besides, the money will be more, and I need it."

"What about me, partner?" asked Tex.

"Miller says there's plenty of work for both of us. I figure we can sell the business easily."

"Sharp, I don't like that idea. We've worked too hard for too many years to give it up."

"You won't go with me, Tex? I thought you and I were partners, no matter what."

"In case you haven't noticed, Tom, I'm old. Besides, you know I met a woman. We's planning on buying a little spread together. I thought I'd work a few more years hauling beef and then retire. But Tom, it won't be the same without you."

"Tex, you won't have any trouble hiring more men to work for you."

"Are you forgettin' I'm a half-breed?"

"No, Tex, but I'm thinking you can deal with that. Like you said, you walk in two worlds."

"Yeah, but one-half of it is ending up on reservations or killed. This is a lousy way to break up, Tom Sharp."

"I'm sorry, Tex, but you got along without me before, and you're better off now."

"When are you leaving?"

"The deal came up sudden like. A while back, I answered an ad for foreman to work cutting poles for a multitelegraph line. It's with the Union Pacific. I just got a message from a John Miller to meet him in Stockton California."

"Then after tomorrow, I'll never see you again?"

"I reckon not. It sure was a fun ride while it lasted."

"That was my line, Tom."

That night they slept in the cabin next to their barn that held freight wagons and horses. In the morning, neither man ate much for breakfast. Tex followed Sharp outside.

"Hate to see you go," said Tex.

"Me too," responded Sharp.

"Then shake my hand, son," said the older man. "There was never a better lad than you."

Tom Sharp had his horse hitched at a rail. Bedroll and full saddlebags tied to the cantle. He went to it and mounted.

"What about the wagons?" asked Tex, looking up at his friend.

"You keep them."

Tex was a hard man all his life and hadn't shed a tear since childhood. This time, looking at his friend ride up the trail and disappear into the trees, the ex-partner watched with tear-filled eyes.

CHAPTER 6

Over the past five years, every three months or so, Tom Sharp sent short messages explaining his progress to the Durretts. Before taking the trail east, he wrote another letter. Unlike the others, it was detailed and lengthy. He explained how he had worked at the meat supply business in California and Oregon mining camps and was now heading to Stockton, California to meet a contractor for the Union Pacific. From there he would head east on another job connected to the railroad. At his next location, he would send a return address. He wondered if the marriage agreement still held. He needed to hear from the parents.

Sharp traveled light and rode south towards California. At Blue Canyon, Sharp met up with a group of five miners he had supplied meat to. The men, in a hurry to take their gold and head for the excitement of San Francisco, traveled hard. In their company there was safety and the group rode as fast as their horses would take them. Sharp reached Stockton in 12 days. It was the early spring of 1867.

Weary, from the hard ride, Tom Sharp took one day to wash up, eat, and rest the night in the hotel where John Miller was staying. In the morning he knocked on his door.

"Mister Miller?"

"Yes, that's me."

"I'm Tom Sharp, you offered me a job?"

"I knew you'd show up," greeted Miller. "Impressive, thirteen days from Blue Canyon to here. I'm ready to go anytime you are. I just purchased the last of my supplies waiting on your arrival. My animals are at the livery. I'll send a boy around to have my packs loaded."

"When I got your message, I traveled as quickly as I could," said Sharp.

"I like a man who is prompt," replied Miller.

Sharp and Miller carried the additional purchases to the livery.

"I try to keep my word," replied Sharp. "Are those three pack mules yours?"

"They sure are. I like to travel in comfort."

"It won't do. Leaving a trail of three shod animals is bad enough, but five? Besides, we need to travel fast and light. If we lose or run out of supplies, we can live off the land."

"Like I said," argued Miller. "I like to travel in comfort."

"You hired me for my knowledge, and with the Indians all riled up about Chivington's attack and the constant immigrants, we'll be lucky to get to where we're going with our hair intact. Two of the pack mules have to go. Best I look through your supplies."

"Sharp, I paid good money for those things."

"I bet you did."

Tom Sharp dismounted and began unstrapping one of the mules. The first thing that came off was a large tent.

"The tent stays," said Miller.

"It'll get you killed," was Sharp's reply.

"I'm not camping each night without a proper shelter."

"Then hire someone else to take you."

"I tried. You're the only educated frontiersman I could find. And I need an educated partner."

"Partner?"

"Fulfilling a government contract for telegraph poles won't be easy. I need a man with knowledge of the country and who can read and write. You'll help me hire men and run a crew. Especially when I'm away ordering supplies and at meetings in Omaha."

"I'll do my best to meet your expectations," replied Sharp. "You can have the tent until we cross the 40 Mile Desert, then you ditch it."

"You expect me to sleep out in the open?"

"A couple blankets and a canvas bedroll will keep you warm and dry, no matter the weather."

"During a storm?"

"Just lift the canvas over your head."

"Huh," replied Miller.

It took Tom Sharp an hour to go over the three pack mules. Extra blankets, clothing, canteens, lanterns, pots, and pans were added to a large pile of unnecessary items. A tight pack of food items remained, including airtights, coffee, one pot, and one pan. The exception was the bulky canvas tent and poles tied above the pack animal's back. Together they returned the two mules and unnecessary supplies. Miller complained about taking a loss.

Sharp purchased two extra pouches of jerky at his own expense, and by noon, they were retracing the trail Tex and Sharp had crossed several years before. Thinking about it, he wouldn't have this job if it wasn't for Tex. That old man had taught him everything he knew about the frontier.

Sharp led the mule up the trail and eastward. John Miller followed.

"You know, after I hired you, I still wondered if you would show up," said Miller. "Sometimes, not many, I've been wrong about an assessment of a man."

"John," said Sharp. "I admit I signed on for the money, but I keep my word. You watch my back on this trip, and I'll watch yours."

"I like that," said Miller. "I was fairly sure I measured you up right. We'll see how it goes. I can't place telegraph poles by myself. The order from the Union Pacific is big, and I'll need a larger crew from now on and you as a partner to help manage them."

"I appreciate the confidence," replied Sharp.

"There's a crew in California that cuts and ships poles to the Central Pacific. The Union Pacific gets their poles and ties from various sources. We'll be one of them, taking down trees in Dakota Territory near Cheyenne. Like I said, part of my job is to take the train back to Omaha for meetings. That's where you come in to run the show."

"What about the current telegraph lines running cross-country?" asked Sharp.

"They'll remain. The first line was in 1861. Communication became instantaneous. That's what put the Pony Express out of business."

"That pony thing was a risky undertaking from the beginning," said Sharp. "I heard it never made a profit. But then, how come a new telegraph line?"

"The new one is a multiline. More efficient to put it along the tracks. It's essential for railroad communication and for ordering supplies. Don't get the idea I run this show. I'm just a subcontractor. But we're doing important work. Important to the railroad and the country."

The two traveled until dusk. Sharp went for wood to make a small fire to heat food and coffee. While Sharp was arranging the fire pit and gathering wood, Miller fooled with his two-man tent. Knowing Sharp wouldn't help, he managed to put it up. It leaned to one side.

"John, I want you to listen to me. For now, I let you have that stupid tent. But like I said, after the desert, it's gone."

"So you said," exclaimed Miller.

"On the prairie, we won't be lighting fires. Light and smoke would give us away. If we're forced to make one, we'll do it quick and then change location."

"I'll do what you say," said Miller. "But it doesn't mean I'll like it."

Before light, Sharp entered the tent and kicked Miller's stocking feet. It was the same way Tex had awakened him all along the trail. It brought a smile to Sharp's face."

"Say," complained Miller. "Can't you wake a man in a normal way?"

"This might save your life," replied Sharp. "I wake you, you jump up, and be ready to go, pronto."

"Aren't you being a bit too…"

"Maybe..."

That morning Sharp waited for his slow-moving boss. He built a quick fire, heated food, and coffee, and immediately put the fire out. It took extra time to load the tent. Back on the trail, Sharp complained.

"That stupid tent takes too long to load. You need to get rid of it."

"No," replied Miller. "I'm the boss. I'm keeping it."

"You were slow this morning. For certain, there will come a time when we have to pack up and move fast. I'm talking from experience. Our lives depend on it."

Miller did not reply.

It was like that every day, and Sharp worried. Miller could not be pushed. It took far too many days to reach the Truckee River. And each day, Miller complained about long hours in the saddle.

"Miller," said Sharp. "Boss or not, I'll tell it like it is. You complain too much. We're about to climb mountains, and the going will be tougher than anything we've done so far. Once we reach the plains, we're going to put in even longer days, dawn to dusk. Why man, we've only done fifteen miles a day. Wagon trains can move faster than that."

"What are you telling me, Sharp?"

"Toughen up!"

Miller didn't reply and said nothing for the rest of the day. At dusk, following the Truckee River, they came to old mining diggings. Debris lined the trail. Remains of dilapidated shacks still stood along the river. There were piles of rock, dirt, and holes along the trail. It was tough on the horses.

"Miners must have been desperate," said Sharp. "Everyone knows the Truckee never showed much gold or silver."

Miller said nothing. They made a cold camp and had jerky and water for supper. They arose early, heated beans and coffee for breakfast, packed, and hit the trail. Riding along the river, they came into a camp of miners. Near a shack, two men stood over a black pot and smoking fire. In the river were Indian women and a line of Indian children, male and female. The adult females' ankles were chained, and the children were tied with rope. Some of the stronger-looking women dug in the river with pickaxes and shovels. Others scooped up the loosened rock and mud. Moving in a continuous circle, chained Indian slaves scooped, carried, and emptied wooden bowls into a gold rocker.

Two guards with rifles stood along the bank. Two other men stood on the river's edge, cracking whips when a child or woman didn't move fast enough. The entire group, whites and Indians, looked ragged and starved.

Sharp caught the attention of a more defiant Indian woman, and he signed. She replied with one hand.

"Watch out," whispered Sharp. "There's six of these white slavers, and there's no way they're going to let us leave. When those two raise their rifles, shoot!"

"What you looking at!" shouted one of the men with a whip. He was the leader, a big dirty man with a long tobacco-stained beard. "There ain't nothing to see. Say, you got supplies on that mule? Whitey! Benny! Let them have it!"

Sharp jumped down, pulling reins with one hand and his rifle with the other. Whitey got off one shot, and the bullet knocked off Miller's hat. Aiming across the saddle, Sharp fired. Miller's mount started bucking, and it leaped towards one of the men with a whip. Its rear hooves raised high and thrust out, sending the slaver backward into the water with a crushed chest.

Sharp's first bullet took Benny in the chest and his second, Whitey, in the head. By then, the three remaining men had pulled pistols and fired. The leader with the whip had no chance to use his weapon. The Indian woman, who made sign to

Sharp, had a pickaxe in her hand, and she swung. Its tip pierced the top of the big man's head. He was dead before he hit the ground. The rest of the Indians bent low in the water as bullets flew. One child, a boy, was struck in the chest and fell back into the rushing stream. Crimson instantly appeared as the child began to float with the current.

Tom Sharp focused on the two remaining men at the cooking pot. Aiming and firing, he did not miss. As quickly as the altercation began, it was over. The Indian woman Sharp signed to waded through the water after the boy, grabbed and carried him onto the bank. The woman called out to the others. The Indians waded through the rushing water to the bank.

John Miller was still fighting his bucking horse.

"Miller!" shouted Sharp. "Pull reins on that damn mount and stop fooling around."

Miller jerked hard on the reins. The iron bit did its job. Dismounting, he sheepishly walked towards Sharp.

"God, man!" exclaimed Miller. "What kind of men can treat children like this?"

"Don't you know?" replied Sharp. "In the first year of the Gold Rush, tens of thousands of Indians were wiped out. The men were killed for bounty or sport, and the women and children were enslaved. It's not pretty, is it?"

"They're starved," said Miller.

"This is where you lose most of your supplies. Take the packhorse to that black pot. We'll start the dry beans cooking. You feed the children airtights, and I'll give the women some jerky. They'll have to wait until the beans are done."

The Indian women and children stood nervously together and watched. Their leader gently laid the dead child on the ground. Sharp, seeing that, went towards her.

Using what sign language Tex had taught him, Sharp tried to communicate.

"Your sign is bad," said the woman. "I speak some English. You not kill us?"

"We will not harm you or the children," replied Sharp.

"You give us food?"

"Yes. Are there more miners?" he asked, pointing to a dead man.

"Two go for food. Four suns ago."

"Maybe some of your people can keep watch?"

The woman spoke, and two females still holding shovels went to either side of the camp to guard.

"Maybe others can help cook?" asked Sharp.

The leader made a gesture, and one woman took over, stirring the raw beans in the black pot.

Another fire was started. Cans of beans were opened and emptied into pans, and heated. The children gathered wooden bowls. They lined up, and Sharp cut the ropes off their ankles. Miller spooned the beans. The women watched in silence. Sharp took jerky from the pack and divided it among the hungry women. He looked at the leader's ankles. They were red and raw. Sharp made sign of striking the iron. The woman smiled. She led Sharp to the wooden shack. Stumbling over one of the dead guards near the cook fire, she motioned. A few of the women dragged the bodies away.

The leader and Sharp entered the shack. It smelled. Filthy blankets lay on cots. In one corner, the woman rummaged. She found a hammer and a chisel. Outside, Sharp found a flat rock. The woman sat on the ground and placed her shackles on it. Sharp, using a hammer and chisel, broke them open. Then Indian women took over and repeated the process.

“Are they finding gold?” asked Sharp to the woman.

“White men fools. No gold here.”

“Then all this was for nothing?” said Sharp.

“We die and starve for nothing.”

Miller, making himself useful, gathered the miner’s weapons. These were placed before the leader.

Together the men tied the pack back on the mule and mounted their horses.

“Take the weapons,” said Sharp, “and protect yourselves and the children.”

“Hard to say thank you to white men,” said the Indian woman.

The two men mounted, and the women and children watched their rescuers ride away.

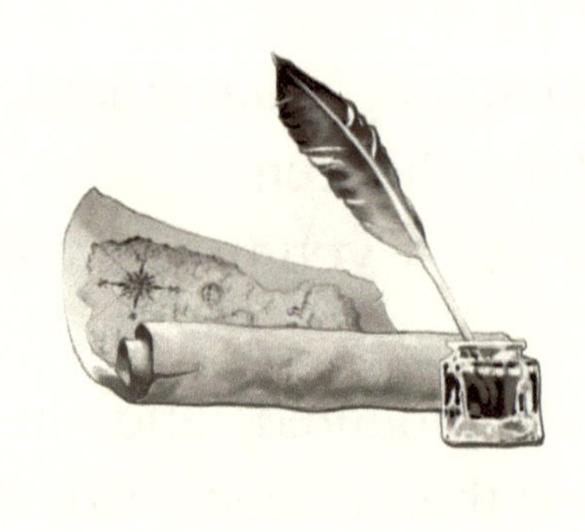

CHAPTER 7

Before dark, they left the trail, found grass, and made a cold camp. Chewing jerky and drinking from a canteen, Miller finally spoke.

"You saved my life back there, and I did nothing."

"Well," replied Sharp. "Your horse got one of them."

Neither man smiled.

"That he did," said Miller. "No thanks to me."

"Still, no telling what that man could have done. Luck was with us."

"That it was," replied Miller. "Do you think those women and kids will make it?"

"The odds are against them. Since the start of the gold rush, Indians have been attacked, killed, or enslaved. In 1851, Burnett, the first governor, called for the total extermination of all Indians in California. In fact, he appropriated a million dollars and put a bounty on their heads. Been going downhill ever since then."

"What a country," said Miller.

"Well...we can't take any consolation. What we're doing with the telegraph and railroad won't make it any better."

"I always said that was progress. First time ever that I thought about it from the other side. We can't stop what's happening to the Indians, but we could be more humane about it."

"I didn't ask specifically," said Sharp. "What happens when we reach Fort Bridger?"

"At the fort, with the help of the railroad, we'll gather more men and supplies. The company put out a call for experienced plainsmen and westerners. We'll also pick up more men, wagons, and equipment in Cheyenne. The Union Pacific is just a short distance from there. It's spring; the railroad ought to reach Cheyenne in November. Right now, they are calling it the Dakota Territory, but I bet in a couple years, it will be named the Territory of Wyoming."

"How do you know this?"

"Nothing goes on in this country, Washington DC doesn't control. Congress keeps those companies close to the vest. Between bonds sold, and for every mile of track laid in the territories, the government will be giving the railroads twenty square miles of land."

"My understanding is that they were given ten square miles," replied Sharp.

"That's true for states," continued Miller. "Railroad gets twenty in territories—like where we're going. We'll be working for those who are making the biggest theft of land and monies since the creation of this country. They are dividing up parts of the US like some kind of chess game."

For once, Miller didn't put up his tent, and the two men laid out their bedrolls and slept under the stars. When Sharp kicked Miller awake in the morning, the fellow seemed to move quicker. The young westerner wondered what he had gotten himself into. Sure, he knew the country; from what Tex had taught him, he was capable. They had to be even more vigilant if they were to make it. Sharp wondered if Miller really could use his weapons. So far, he hadn't. But then, his horse did kill that feller. Sharp smiled.

"I'm curious, can you really use that Henry and Colt you're carrying?"

"I can," replied Miller.

"From now on, until Fort Bridger, no more cooking fires. The rest of the way, we'll be living off jerky and water. Besides, we don't have much food left anyway."

"Confound it, Sharp. I want a hot meal and coffee!"

"Then here's where we split up. I don't want to be killed by you refusing to follow my lead."

"All right, all right, Sharp. But I'm not going to like this one bit."

"It's not a question of liking. We'll be two raggedy, saddle-sore hombres by the time we reach Fort Bridger. Look at those peaks ahead. It'll be cold and tough going."

"As you say," said Miller.

With a blanket around him, each man faced blowing wind and snow and pushed east through the mountains.

Eventually, they came to the 40 Mile Desert and crossed through to the Humboldt River. Miller was once again obstinate and insisted on putting up his tent. Sharp caught the man taking water from the stagnant stream and beginning to drink.

"There's dead animals in that stream. For that matter, maybe a few humans somewhere upriver. You really want to get this far and die?"

Sharp took the pot and pan and filled both with water. Over a small fire, he boiled the liquid and filled the canteens. Miller, thirsty, was barely able to wait until the water cooled.

"Get more water, boil it, and fill the other canteens. And Miller…"

"Yeah?"

"Quit taking chances."

Sharp made camp in tall brush, some distance from the river. That night, sullen and surly, John Miller went to his tent. Sharp was uneasy. Some instinct told him trouble was coming. As tired as he was, the westerner laid out his bedroll and made it look like a sleeping person. He faded into the dark to keep watch.

The westerner sat on a rock, holding his Henry, and thought about his boss. We should have moved on. Miller's too tired and ornery to push. Tomorrow, I've got to take that stupid tent away from him. That'll be a scene. The 40 Mile Desert nearly did him in. He might be a good businessman, but he's no frontiersman.

Past midnight, Sharp slid off the rock and sat down. Still cradling the rifle in his arms, he leaned back and slept.

Sun on his face, Tom Sharp opened his eyes. Sitting up, he looked at the tent's front flap, its grayish-white color showing conspicuously on the beige land. Near the tent lay his bedroll and saddle. To the right, the hobbled animals were grazing, heads bent.

Far off, the clip-clop of horse hooves could be heard. Kneeling down behind the large boulder, rifle thrust forward, Sharp waited. Through the brush, he saw two blue uniforms, one big man and the other a short skinny fellow. The larger soldier was wearing sergeant stripes.

"How's come youse always ridin' and I walk, Sarge? How's come?"

"If you hadn't given me that bottle, and I hadn't got drunk and hit that loo-ten-it, we's wouldn't be deserters. That's why you be walkin'."

"But it was you that stole the whiskey from me."

"No matter, boy, it was your whiskey that got me in trouble."

"I don't like this one bit, Henry. I mean...Sarge."

"Huh, you'll like it and live with it, or else. Well…looky there, Patty, two hosses and a mule!"

"Now's I don't have to walk."

"Shhhh, boy! There's someone about."

Sharp watched as the sergeant dismounted, tied his US mount to a bush, and pulled a pistol from a fasten-down holster.

"I thought so," whispered the deep bass voice of the sergeant. "See, there's some fool in a tent and another lying on the ground yonder. And look, a pack of supplies!"

"I see 'em, Sarge."

"Shhh, now Patty, when I go to open that tent flap, you shoot that feller on the ground. Now mind you, don't miss. We be needin' that pack."

"Should I ought to, Sarge? Can't we just…"

"Do as I say!" hissed the sergeant.

Both soldiers, pistols in hand, stepped quietly toward their prey. The skinny fellow walked near the bedroll and stopped. He turned and watched the sergeant go to the tent. When he touched the flap, the younger soldier fired his pistol twice into the blanketed bundle on the ground. Sharp, his rifle held steady across the boulder, called out.

"Hey, stupid! I'm over here."

The young soldier turned, and Sharp fired. Inside the tent, Miller awoke. He reached back and took his Colt from under his pillow. The tent flap opened, and coming towards him was a big man with a pistol. The soldier pointed it at Miller and Miller fired first. The sergeant staggered out, still holding his Army Colt. His other hand was on his chest. John Miller appeared at the front of the tent opening. He was in stocking feet, fully dressed, and holding a smoking revolver. He saw the sergeant begin to raise his weapon, and Miller fired again. The big man twisted on his feet and fell.

"John!" said Sharp, grinning. "Morning. Glad to see you're awake."

"Tom Sharp, I don't think that's one bit funny."

"Well, you proved you can shoot."

Without discussion, the two sojourners placed the supply pack on the mule and together tied it down. They blanketed and saddled their horses and removed hobbles and ropes. They took the tack off the US Cavalry mount and let it run free. Tying down bedrolls, they mounted and rode off. The grayish tent stood brightly in the sun's glare, and the two dead deserters lay on the ground where they fell.

CHAPTER 8

At noon, the men stopped to eat jerky and share one last airtight of peaches.

"I'm beginning to see what you mean about paying attention on the trail," commented Miller.

"I thought you might," said Sharp and smiled. "At least you got rid of that stupid tent."

"Yeah, all I want to do is get to Fort Bridger.

"John," began Sharp. "After all you said about the railroad, can you trust them to pay?"

"They need the poles and the telegraph. If we deliver on time, they'll pay."

"Good. The way you explained it, everyone involved with the railroad is a bunch of crooks."

Miller laughed at that.

"From that perspective, they are," he said. "Let me add something I've been meaning to say. There is a lot about the railroad I bet you don't know, both the Central Pacific and Union Pacific, but you'll learn. Before this ends, I bet you'll wish you were working with the Central Pacific. The Chinese are a lot less rowdy than the Irish."

"Just as long as I get paid, I've learned to handle tough situations."

"That's why I hired you. A fellow that knows the West and how to wield a weapon. I think you proved that."

"I reckon," replied Sharp, and he smiled, "glad you're learning how to stay alive out here."

It was now some three hundred miles to Fort Bridger. The two travelers pushed their ponies and the pack mule hard. Sometimes they made forty miles a day. Both men became fiercely hungry, ragged, and saddle sore. Still, they rode on. One night, Sharp wondered what kind of luck it was that they picked a likely place to camp, and there lay the parts of the three dead men. The filthy scavengers, he, Tex, and the breed's horse killed.

"I see three skulls," said Miller. "Let's move on and find another place. I wonder whether they were whites or Indians."

"Does it matter?" asked Sharp. "They're dead."

"Hate to see white folks murdered like that."

"Maybe they deserved it," replied Sharp.

"Why do you say that?"

"Not all white men are good."

"Sometimes, Sharp, you make me wonder. Have you always run into renegades in your travels?"

"Matter of fact, I have."

They traveled further north and east to reach Fort Bridger.

"I should warn you, Miller. We're close to the fort. My experience is there will be tribes of Indians camped near it."

Tex's words rang in his head. How he missed his friend.

"Why is that?" asked Miller.

"Indians are people. They want tobacco and supplies just like everyone else. They also like to trade and bet on horse races."

"You're worried I'll do something wrong."

"Just don't stare or act like a greenhorn."

"Doesn't seem you have much confidence in…"

Again, Sharp smiled, and he made sure Miller saw it.

"When we started, you were an ignoramus on the trail. I'm just preparing you. You've come a long way since those first days."

"Thanks, Sharp. How much do we have to worry about Indians when cutting poles?"

"A lot. I've said it before. If anything, the Indians are more riled than ever. The Chivington Massacre at Sand Creek in '64 proved to the tribes that they would never be safe from whites. It's a miracle the peace chief, Black Kettle survived. It's worse with the killing of buffs for hides and tongues. And I don't have to tell you what the railroad means to the tribes."

"It's the Sioux we worry about?" asked Miller.

"It's all of them," answered Sharp. "Where we're going, it's the Bannock and Shoshone. Further on, it will be the Arapaho, Cheyenne, and Sioux. And south, are the Commanche, Kiowa, and Apaches. Since the massacre with Chivington, all the tribes have been talking to each other. And they sure don't think highly of whites."

"And your point is?"

"At the fort, if the two of us are going to stay out of trouble, we watch and keep our mouths shut. The men you hire have to do the same. Make sure to pick up some good plainsmen. Our survival depends on that."

"I'll leave the hiring to you."

"After we leave the fort, we'll have to move fast. We've been in the heart of Indian country for sometime now."

"You're really worried, aren't you?" asked Miller.

"The tribes might be friendly at the fort but not so away from it. After Fort Bridger, with more men, it'll be even harder to get through to Cheyenne."

The last day on the trail, they made a cold camp and hit their bedrolls early. At daybreak, Sharp saw a group of Shoshone warriors in the distance. There were more than thirty of them on horseback and traveling fast.

"No time," said Sharp, kicking Miller's feet. "Indian war party."

Running, Sharp gathered the three animals and dragged them into camp. He saddled the horses and tied down the panniers on the back of the pack mule.

"Hurry!" ordered Sharp.

John Miller was still waking up and stomping into boots when Sharp handed him reins.

"We'll walk the horses north and try to stay to low ground. Follow me and be quiet."

Sharp had no illusions. The Shoshone would be hard to avoid. Stepping to a run, leading his mount and the packhorse, he found rocky ground and stayed on it. It led up and over a steep incline. Looking back, Sharp could make out war paint on Indian ponies. So far, the warriors didn't see them. Miller turned his head, and for the first time, he caught sight of the Indians. Suddenly, his slow demeanor transformed, and he ran in earnest, pulling the reins of his horse.

Descending, they came onto an outcropping of granite. Clopping horses' hooves and booted feet left no tracks.

The Creator is looking out for us, thought Sharp.

The two men mounted with a ridge of rock and earth behind them. The solid shelf of rock ended. Sharp pushed his animals into a dead run. Picking hard-packed ground, he continued on. They rode for hours, avoiding the Indians. Finally, they came to a copse of trees and rode through thick brush. On the other side, they found a pond and watered their horses. Mounting, they rode on and, in the late afternoon, came to the fort.

"You can thank God and that rocky ground. It saved our lives. This morning you fell back to your old ways. Don't do it again."

Miller's reply was one long exasperated sigh. He followed Sharp's back and the rump of his pack mule toward the fort. They rode through Indian encampments of Shoshone, Bannock, and Paiute. Sharp wondered if some of the Shoshone watching their arrival were part of the war party they encountered.

Inside the fort they met a group of immigrants and hangers-on, hard men of all ages and manner of dress. There was one old-timer who still carried a Hawken rifle. He wore a long beard and hair, a leather band around his head, and a wide belt over dark, smoke-stained buckskins. On his feet were heavy moccasins.

"Hello there, I'm Tom Sharp. You looking for work?"

"A feller has to have coin to eat," responded the old man.

"What do you call yourself?" asked Sharp.

"Now, dependin' on the mood, mostly fair words, but in hard times I curse myself out good."

"This being one of those hard times?"

"I reckon. Pelts get no price, can't haul enough meat on my back for profit, and as much as I like my cabin up yonder, a feller's got to have a nest egg to keep goin'."

"That's why you're here?"

"It is. You pay fair wages, and you got yourself a worker."

"What handle do you want me to use?"

"Call me Smoke."

"All right, Smoke," said Sharp, smiling and extending his hand. "Shake, you got yourself a job."

The handshake was as expected. Firm and nearly bone-crushing. The old man was no doubt twice as strong as his younger counterpart. A lifetime of hard living and surviving in the wilderness made him that way.

"What will I be doing, Sharp?"

"Mostly scouting and giving advice," replied the younger man. "Where's the best place to cut poles, where to find meat, and how to deal with the Indians."

"Say," said Smoke. "There's more to you than what appears on the surface."

"I've been around," answered Sharp.

"What are you doing talking to this old man?" asked John Miller, annoyed. "Help me decide which of these fellows is up to hard work."

"John Miller, meet Smoke. This old man, as you call him, knows the country. His knowledge will save both of us a lot of grief."

"Did you hire him?" asked Miller.

"I did, and he gets top wages. Fifty-five dollars a month. He's our scout, and he does no hard labor. It's his advice and knowledge we're after."

"Sharp," said Miller. "I hope you know what you're doing."

"You hired me for my experience, didn't you? Well…Smoke knows more about this country, where good timber, game, and the Indians are... than we'll ever know in two lifetimes. We need him more than he needs us."

With that, Smoke laughed and then took out a pipe and a leather tobacco pouch. Within a short time, smoke was curling around his head.

"How could you know all that?" asked Miller. "You just met him."

"Just see if what I said isn't true," retorted Sharp.

The old plainsman found a crate to sit on and build a smoke. He watched as Miller and Sharp interviewed the younger men. Some clearly were not up to hard labor. Some were smelly drunks and riff-raff. Out of about thirty, the two contractors for the Union Pacific Railroad picked seven men.

***

Cheyenne lay some three hundred miles due east as the crow flies. The entire way was now patrolled by riled warriors. The skill of the old frontiersman got the party of ten through Indian country.

True to Miller's contract, in Cheyenne, wagons, men, money, and supplies were waiting. The newly hired pole-cutters traveled east on horseback and on four large freight wagons as a group. Smoke led them to the advancing party of Irish railroad workers. Briefly, they watched the laying of ties and rails. The noise was deafening, their ears constantly bombarded by the incessant pounding of sledgehammers on steel. Further down the track was the famous Hell-on-Wheels encampment, the crooked money grubbers Sharp had heard so much about.

John Miller searched and located the railroad foreman. Beside him was a group of surveyors and their equipment.

"Are you John Griffen, foreman?"

"Who's asking?"

"John Miller, I have a contract to cut telegraph poles for the Union Pacific."

"We've been waiting on you. You're a week late."

"It's a miracle we're here at all. We had Indian trouble."

"I don't want excuses, Miller. Get your crew to cutting and hauling poles."

"Mr. Griffen, it's a new crew, but we'll get the job done."

Smoke led the pole-cutters to a large timber growth near the railroad. The crew began felling trees that were suitable for telegraph poles. These they trimmed and loaded onto the wagons. Sharp and Miller helped the pole cutters develop a routine on the first day. They rotated cutting, trimming, and hauling the poles, ensuring there was always a full load going and returning from the tracks. Once delivered, the telegraph crews dug and placed them. Immediately the multi-wire lines were strung and connected. Now, the railroad foreman had instant communication with Omaha.

***

John Miller was right. The Irish were rowdy, and the Chinese were not. As Miller explained it, the Chinese were grateful for the work. With sheer will, they carved their way through the mountains with hammers, chisels, and black powder. Earning thirty dollars a month, they sent money back to families in California or China.

On the other hand, Miller explained that the Irish received fifty dollars a month. Unfortunately, work on the Union Pacific was hampered by gamblers, prostitutes, and makeshift bars. There was a reason they called the temporary settlements behind the advancing tracks 'Hell on Wheels.' The workers drank, fought, and whored all night. The rowdy Irish got their money lifted as fast as they earned it. Not all the Irish workers were like that, but far too many were.

Smoke and Sharp were both disgusted with the mean smelly workers and the noisy camp. They became fast friends, and each night they traveled as far as they could out onto the open prairie to sleep, sleep the two men so badly needed.

During the day, Sharp continued to seek better ways to cut and haul telegraph poles. Smoke guarded the crew and constantly scouted for Indians. Incessantly, the various railroad laborers were harassed and attacked by Indians. During these attacks, the workers were provided with weapons. More than a thousand rifles were kept in train cars for emergencies.

For the pole cutters, it was back-breaking work, cutting, loading, and hauling. The same for railroad workers. It didn't take but a few weeks to find that food supplies were always a problem for the Union Pacific. The beef they hauled in by railroad was insufficient. The herd of cattle they kept alongside the railroad to cut up by the butcher car, was often stolen or run off by Indians. Sharp appointed one of the crew for extra money to boss the pole cutters. He and Smoke hired additional men to go with him to shoot and haul in buffalo meat. They used work wagons the railroad provided for their hungry and complaining workers.

"These Irish are heavy eaters," said Miller.

"If you dug in the dirt, hauled ties and rails all day, you'd have an appetite too," replied Sharp.

"Hauling and digging holes for these poles isn't exactly easy, partner."

"No, John, but those Irish have the tougher job."

"I see the railroad pays us by the amount of meat you bring daily," said Miller.

"I'm borrowing more railroad freight teams and wagons and ordering more salt. And I need to find some experienced shooters. Fresh meat doesn't last long, and we've got to make a stand, shoot, dress out, salt, and load it into the wagons."

"The railroad boss appreciates what you do," exclaimed John Miller.

"I don't have to tell you, but I will. The Cheyenne, Arapaho, and Sioux don't take kindly to the railroad. Worse, they know what it will bring. I need more men who can shoot quick and move fast in case of trouble."

"That's why you take extra horses tied to the wagons?"

"Yes. Smoke and I worked that out. If attacked, it's the only way to escape. The railroad can replace the horse teams, wagons, and meat, but not our hides."

"We're making history here, Tom," said Miller. "If this work was easy other men would be doing it. It takes fellows like you and me, willing to take risks financially and with our lives to get the job done. The railroad and the multiline telegraph will open up this country, transform it, and project the nation into a modern future."

"At the expense of those who were here first. The Indians will fight us to our last breath."

"Perhaps so, but we'll win. There are more of us, we have the better weapons, and nothing can stop progress."

"That's where you and I differ," replied Tom Sharp. "We've discussed this before. I'm doing this to buy a ranch to raise horses and cattle. But it doesn't mean I have to like it."

"No? Well, partner, just keep on working. Go out there and get that meat and feed these workers. Earn more money for both of us. If you get shot at, shoot back. Like I said, if it was easy, weaker men than us would be out here, and the pay would be less."

"So you've forgotten what we encountered on the trail?"

"No," replied Miller. "I've thought about those women and kids. Those white men were animals. The difference between them and us is that what we are doing is progress. And, regarding the Indian situation, they are on the wrong end of this. And long as they stay that way, they'll suffer."

"I'm going now," said Sharp. "I'm meeting a group of westerners I wired to join the hunters. If they pan out, we'll be bringing in more buffalo meat."

"That's the spirit," laughed Miller. "You don't have to like taking from the Indians, but if we don't do it, someone else will."

Tom Sharp greeted and hired more men. Four large freight wagons and teams traveled north. A half a day's journey from the railroad, they encountered buffalo. Halting, the experienced hunters split up, found a herd, and made their stands from a distance. The accurate Sharps rifles were powerful enough to bring down a buff with one well-placed shot. Sometimes only a few could be harvested before the big animals stampeded. Other times, with the leaders of the herd picked off, buffalo continued grazing while nearly an entire group of fifty or more big buffs were brought down.

Eventually, this fatal flaw of not running away would be the buffalo's demise. Tom Sharp could see it, yet millions of buffs still roamed the western plains. Sharp didn't like that the men shot more than they could cut up and haul. He made up for it by ordering at least the tongues of every animal, a delicacy, to be cut out, salted, and placed in a wagon. But still, it was an awful gory mess to see buffalo carcasses lying dead on the prairie. This would certainly further rile the Indians.

One night the four wagons came in after dark, filled with salted buffalo meat and tongues. It was a lot to process, and when Sharp led the wagons to the butcher car, the meat cutters complained.

"Mister Sharp," said the head butcher, "we don't get paid enough to cut up this meat all hours of the night."

"Want to tell the railroad boss that?" asked Sharp.

"Nawww, no need to bother him. But at least your men can help load that stuff into our meat car."

Sharp gave orders. His men complied and took the wagons and teams to where they would bed down for the night. That evening, Smoke and

Sharp walked their horses across the tracks. They headed for a likely knoll to sleep away from the noisy camp. Even at ten o'clock, the Irish were drinking, gambling, and carrying on. Loud shouts, an occasional gunshot, music, and singing reached the disgusted ears of the two westerners.

In the dark, they came up to three big Irishmen. One was holding a whiskey bottle; two others were pushing a young woman in a filthy dress. The men were laughing, and the girl, appearing very young under the moon and starlight, was sobbing. It was Smoke who reacted first. He was carrying that old Hawken of his, cradled in his arms like a baby.

"Here now," said Smoke. "That'll be enough of that."

"Who says so?" asked the man with the bottle. "We be just havin' a wee bit of fun."

"That girl looks like a child," said Smoke. "She's crying! Leave her be!"

"Or what?" asked the Irishman.

The other two smelly and filthy railroad men stopped pushing the girl, stood drunkenly, and stared. Tom Sharp moved quickly, grabbed the girl's wrist, and pulled her behind himself and Smoke.

"This here rifle," said the plainsman, "is old, but this .56 caliber will blow your head clean off."

"Try it, Mister," said the man with the bottle.

"That's enough sassing," growled Smoke, setting his rifle down and pulling what looked like a large butcher knife. "I changed my mind. I'm gonna cut you up with my Green River knife. It won't be my first time leaving a man's guts on the prairie."

The big man threw the half-empty bottle away, and they heard smashing glass. His two companions complained. Smoke advanced, and so did the drunken man, a broad grin on his face. A quick flash of steel and a long line of crimson appeared on the left arm of the Irishman. He squealed out in pain.

"You cut me!"

"You asked for it," said Smoke. "Now take your two stupid friends and git!"

Smoke didn't know it, but behind him, Sharp had one hand on the wrist of the girl and, in his right, his Colt revolver.

"We be leavin'," said the Irishman holding his bleeding arm. "But it ain't us you be dealin' with. So's you know, we paid for that hussy."

"Yeah," said another of the three men. "Irish Mike owns that there gal, and he'll be coming for her. And he'll stomp both of you into the ground for interfering with his business."

The railroad workers disappeared into the dark.

"Who is this Irish Mike?" asked Smoke, turning to the girl.

"You have to let me go," replied the young woman's voice. "I'll get a beating for this."

"It wasn't your fault," said Tom Sharp.

"Just the same, it'll happen."

"How old are you, girl?" asked Smoke.

"That doesn't matter either," was the reply.

"It does to us," said Sharp. "You're not going back. Not tonight. Suppose you follow. We're making camp out on the prairie away from that noise. You have nothing to fear."

"I know you're trying to help, but you're making it worse for me. I'll be in…"

"If you're a mind to go back and take a beatin'," said Smoke, "we won't interfere. But if you want to be free of this here, then follow us. Let her go, Sharp. It's up to her."

Sharp let go of the girl's wrist he had held onto all this time. He went back in the dark and came forward with their horses. Smoke took his horse's reins, and both men started walking into the night away from the railroad noise. After a few steps, they heard a faint word.

"Wait," said the girl.

Sharp and Smoke stopped, and slowly the young female advanced.

"If I don't go back tonight, they'll search for me tomorrow. Irish Mike or his men will kill me if they find me."

"As long as I live," said Smoke, in as kind a voice as Sharp ever heard, "no one will be hurtin' you, gal. Never again. And that's a promise."

"But how will you keep it?" she asked, her voice trembling.

"What's your name?" asked Sharp.

"Hilda Regenschirm."

"Once we make camp and get you something to eat and drink," said Smoke, "you can tell us how you got yourself into this mess. That is, if'n you're up to it."

The two men found a knoll, went around it, and discovered a cleared area. The noise from the railroad was greatly diminished. They made a hand-sized fire and cooked a choice bit of buffalo meat. Handing the girl a tin plate, a fork, and a knife, Smoke pointed to a large boulder. The girl sat down and ate hungrily, cutting the meat with great vigor. When she finished, they handed her a tin cup of hot coffee. Blowing on it, she sipped noisily, and the two plainsmen smiled. The men ate silently, and Sharp cleaned the utensils and packed them away. He put the fire out with sand. They watched white smoke rise up into the star-filled sky. Far in the background, coyotes competed with the noise from the railroad camp.

"It's hard to trust anyone," said Hilda. "But I do appreciate what you did for me back there. Those men were sure going to use me. I…"

"Just tell it as it comes to you," said Smoke.

"My folks are from Germany. We're second generation. My mother, sisters, and brothers back in New York…well…we struggled. My father worked for the railroad, and he was injured. He eventually died. We had it good, and then, not… We had to move. To a worse part of town. I took a job in a bar and…"

"And this Irish Mike found you and took you," interjected Smoke.

"That's it," said Hilda. "He forced me. He and his men. I still refused to be that way, but he beat me. The slightest thing, and I was hit."

The girl began to cry. She took in great sobbing breaths. Smoke and Sharp sat on their bedrolls across from the girl and waited. Slowly the heavy breathing and crying stopped. There was a long silence.

"I hate it," said the girl. "I'm so ashamed. I can never go back to my mother. She wouldn't understand. And I don't want to... Maybe it would have been better if you would have let those men kill me. It's all I..."

"If you want a better life, girl," said Smoke, "it starts here. I don't promise it will be easy. The West never is. But you can have it if you're willin' to work for it."

"What do you have in mind?" asked Sharp.

"We can place her with Mrs. White and the wash crew she has. She'll protect her and call on us if she needs help. What do you say, girl?" asked Smoke. "Do you think you could wash clothes for a living? Until something else comes along?"

"Anything is better than what I was doing," said Hilda, wiping tears away with her hand.

"In the morning," said Sharp, "we'll take you to Mrs. White. She's a hard-working and fair-minded lady. She has a work crew that boils up laundry for the camp. Hard but clean work. I'll pay her to get you out of that dress and into some decent clothes. That'll be a start."

"Why are you being so kind to me?" asked Hilda. "You don't even…"

"I have a daughter your age," said Smoke. "No decent man would see a young girl abused. I have an extra canvas and a blanket. You sleep close by, and in the morning, we'll git you situated."

It was as Smoke said. Mrs. White was firm but fair when Smoke spoke to her privately about the young girl.

"Poor lass is no more than sixteen, I venture," said Mrs. White. "I'll take her to the wagon, get her a bath and clean clothes. We'll burn that filthy thing she's wearing. If this Irish Mike or his men come 'round, I have a man with a shotgun, and I have this."

From somewhere in her large and ample dress, she produced a derringer.

"We'll be visiting," said Smoke. "If the girl's a mind, she can join my family up in the territory when I quit this affair. My woman and my girls would be welcoming."

With that, Sharp and Smoke went back to scouting and searching for buffalo.

***

Each day out on the prairie seemed like an eternity. There was danger for the pole cutters and the railroad crew every step of the way. From time to time, disease swept through the large Union Pacific camp. There was very little medical care, and men died. The filthy gambling camps brought chaos and further worsened the situation. Repeatedly, the workers endured Indian attacks from the angry Cheyenne. There were armed guards, but hardly enough for a large, sustained attack.

Tom Sharp learned not to take his meat wagons too far from the railroad or risk losing everything to hostiles. Already he had several minor brushes with the Indians, but his skilled shooters held them off, and they were able to load meat onto the wagons and return to the ever-moving railroad camp. But it was inevitable that such luck would not hold.

Too many days had gone by without finding buffalo. The beef shipped by rail was insufficient to meet the needs of the railroad crew. Another herd of beef cattle was recently run off by a group of Cheyenne. Pressure was put on Sharp to take the wagons further out in search of the roaming buffalo herds. The westerner insisted each man have a personal horse tied to the back of the wagon team, as well as Henry repeaters along with their Sharp rifles. Cautiously, they moved north across the prairie. Miles from camp, they finally spotted a large herd. Stopping and moving forward on foot, the hunters divided, found grazing buffalo, and set up shooting stands. With the first ongoing volley of shots from .52 caliber Sharps, a large party of Cheyenne appeared, riding furiously towards the hunters.

"Escape to your horses!" yelled Sharp.

In unison, the entire hunting party ran towards the guarded wagon teams. Sharp and Smoke reached the wagons first. They climbed up top of one and began using the single-shot rifles. Both knocked leading Cheyenne Warriors from their saddles. Jumping down, the former Confederate soldier ran to his horse and removed his Henry. Climbing back up on the wagon, the skilled shooter did not miss. Every .44 caliber rimfire bullet struck an attacking warrior, and Indian saddles were emptied. In this,

Smoke was no competition with his single shot Hawkins.

"Old man," yelled Sharp, "get your horse and go."

Reluctantly, Smoke climbed down and yelled a reply, "Watch who you're calling old."

Still, the frontiersman complied, and mounting, he yelled back.

"Keep your hair, youngen!"

The war party was a big one. Sharp watched as two of his men were shot down and trampled by Cheyenne horses. The other hunters untied their mounts and raced toward camp. Sharp was the last to leave, his rifle empty. He jumped on his horse, a racer with hot blood mixed with mustang. He caught up with Smoke and his men. Taking the lead, he led them on the long ride to camp. Looking behind, Sharp saw smoke, and already yellow flame was rising from the heavy freight wagons, the large teams unharnessed by the Indians.

The main body of the Cheyenne war party continued the long chase, and when the hunters came near the railroad, Sharp drew his Army Colt and fired three quick shots in warning. Ahead he saw men running, the camp in real chaos. Guards climbed to firing positions along a waiting steam engine while workers were handed rifles. That day, the camp was overrun. Many railroad laborers were killed, and the track behind the train was torn up by the Indians. Telegraph lines were cut. It was not the first Indian attack, and it would not be the last before the Transcontinental Railroad would be completed.

***

Word came to Sharp from one of his frontiersmen that the Union Pacific was hiring a large party of Pawnee to patrol and protect the railroad and telegraph lines. He sought out his partner and told him the news.

"Why didn't they do it sooner?" asked Sharp.

"Beats me," replied John Miller. "I suspect money has something to do with it. We've been asking Sherman to supply troops, but he's been slow to act. I heard he promised to send five thousand. You know they're building that Fort Russell some miles from Cheyenne, but God only knows when it's finished or when soldiers come."

"I lost two men today," said Sharp. "Chasing after those moving buffalo is not easy."

Chapter 8

"I reckon not," said Miller. "But you do all of us a big service. A man has to eat."

***

Two weeks later, after spending a restless night, Tom Sharp got up early. He ate breakfast and put together his personal items, and packed them on his horse. He first sought out the frontiersman.

"I've had my fill," said Sharp to his friend Smoke.

"I saw you had no stomach for killing them buffs and shooting Indians," said Smoke. "Matter of time afore I knew you'd pull out. A man has to stick to his convictions."

"Smoke," said Sharp. "You're the one thing in this entire chaotic mess I'm going to miss."

"Same here, friend," replied the older man. "But me, I have no choice. This will be my last stand with a mess of noisy humans. I got to put together as much coin as I can before heading back to my cabin. Purtiest little place you've ever seen. I miss my woman and family."

"I bet," said Sharp.

"I was gonna tell, ya..." began the frontiersman.

"Yes?"

"Mrs. White came running last night when we got back. She said her shotgun man was elsewhere, and she needed help. You disappeared, so I went with her. When we got to her wash wagon, two men were dragging Hilda away."

"Well?" asked Sharp.

"That washer woman ain't all talk. She put one of those fellers away with that little hideaway gun. Right in the forehead."

"And?"

"They was right about Irish Mike. He was one big tough fellow."

"Go on…"

"Well…let's just say there was a lot of him to carve up. He won't be bothering Hilda no more."

"That's how you got that bruise on your face? What did you do with the bodies?"

"Mrs. White had some old canvas. I went after one of the work wagons, and she and I lifted those fellers in the back and took a trip out on the prairie. Except for Hilda, it seems no one saw us. The workers were at supper."

"I'm glad the girl's safe," said Sharp. "But she must not favor working for…"

"We discussed it," said Smoke. "Hilda wants to get away. After a few more months saving coin, she and I are heading back to my cabin. My Shoshone woman and daughters will be glad to have the company."

"She won't mind living in the wilderness?"

"Hilda said she'll be happy to get away from people. She says she's looking forward to it. Told me she wants to learn to hunt and fish."

"I'm glad," said Sharp. "For both of you."

The two westerners shook hands. Smoke watched Tom Sharp walk away, leading his horse to where John Miller kept his tent. Smoke reluctantly turned his head. The old man found himself surprised to think, at least for a moment, that he wished he had no obligations and was young enough to go with his friend.

Sharp went to his boss's tent and pulled back the flap. Miller was inside, sitting at a table doing paperwork.

"John," said Sharp. "I'm tired of killing and seeing my men picked off by Indians. And, to tell the truth, I'm tired of leaving bloody buff carcasses lying on the prairie, their meat half harvested. It's been a week since I've found a buffalo herd close to the train line. All we've been doing is riling the Indians even more than before. I'm giving notice. I'm going."

"When?"

"Right now."

"I can't talk you out of it, Tom?"

"No."

"You're leaving me up short. But I can't say I haven't seen it coming. I don't remember the last time I saw you smile. Go then, if you have to. It's hard to find a man of your ability. You're going to be difficult, if not impossible, to replace. But it's a good thing you hired Smoke. Something tells me I'm going to be relying on him from now on."

"Glad you see it that way. That mountain man needs the money, and his knowledge surpasses mine," said Sharp. "I appreciate what you've done for me, John. But as I told you from the beginning, I don't like what we're doing to the Indians. Taking their land without fair compensation is wrong. I bet there isn't one promise our government, the railroad, or the Army has made to them that has been kept."

"Reckon not, Tom. But that's progress. Sorry to see you leave. Here, take this envelope. I'm paying you out of ready cash. I'm riding the train back to Omaha for a meeting in the morning. If you don't mind, I'll shake your hand now, partner."

Before mounting his horse, Sharp looked at the envelope Miller had handed him. It felt thicker than usual. Inside was more than three times what he was owed. Smiling, Tom Sharp climbed up on his saddle. John Miller opened his tent flap and, with deep remorse, surreptitiously watched Sharp ride away from the noise of the railroad workers and the unending pounding of sledgehammers on steel. Miller stared at the retreating rider for some time, suddenly realizing that perhaps Tom Sharp was a caliber of man he would never meet again.

CHAPTER 9

The Union Pacific tracks were still being laid across the Dakota Territory. Now, it was miles closer to Cheyenne. It was at that point Sharp split from his job. Riding carefully through Indian country, he realized he wouldn't miss working for the railroad. *Miller's a good man,* thought Sharp, *but far too greedy for his own good. Still, isn't money and fortune the very ingredient I'm searching for? I know money is not enough. Smoke has it right; a man must have a family to be complete.*

Sharp smiled grimly, his money belt much heavier than before. He traveled north, keeping to low ground, avoiding Indians, wanting to see the country. He rode for days, glad to be alone for the first time in years. He reflected perhaps he'd take one more job before purchasing horses and heading south to find a ranch. Katherine and her folks wouldn't wait forever.

Riding up into British Columbia, he was surprised to see buffs and learn there was another species, the Wood Buffalo. An old-time fur trapper he traveled a short way with told him about the animals.

"You want to know about them wood buffalo? Third again, as large as the plains. Why they's roam up into the Yukon, Alaska, and the Northwest Territories. They're even up in Alberta. They's got short legs and more weight to 'em. Tough creatures scraping deep snow with their big heads for grass in the winter."

"Have you seen them yourself, old timer?" asked Sharp.

"Sure have. But the way them gold miners and immigrants are shootin' em, won't be none left afore too long."

"For fifty bucks, would you take me to see at least one of them?"

"Heap of money," said the old-timer. "I don't know you. Why fer should I take you? You gonna shoot one?"

"No, I've had my fill of seeing naked carcasses rot in the open air. I quit a job because I realized how wrong it is."

"Well, I suppose I could lead you up north. I was headin' in that direction anyways. But if I take you to one, you best not be shootin', or I'll…"

"No worries, old man. I give my word."

Sharp put out his hand, and the old man laughed, spit in his, and then shook with bone-crushing strength.

They traveled north, taking their time, living off the land. Finally, they encountered one old male Wood Buffalo in a low hidden valley.

"There she be, Sharp," said the old man.

"Thank you, Dawson," Sharp replied and paid the old timer in gold.

"Suppose you go up to that old woody and tell him to go off and start a herd. Be purely shameful to lose the likes of him. So long, feller. With young men like you, perhaps there is hope for this country after all."

Sharp watched the old feller ride away. Dismounting, the young man observed the largest buffalo he had ever seen. He watched it graze and occasionally lift and shake its magnificent head. It was a big hairy beast. The former buff hunter sat down. He rested and observed the large fellow forage. For once, Sharp lazed through the afternoon

and made camp on a piece of ground, cleared and scraped by the shaggy beast. The big fellow was absolutely magnificent. Finally, Sharp stepped forward and spoke to the animal.

"Hello, old fellow. You're out here all alone, just like me. Sometimes, we just have to get away, don't we? Once in a while, one needs to gather thoughts and enjoy the quiet solitude. Isn't that so? Bet you're wandering around wondering what you will do next. Or maybe you have a plan to meet up with some of your kind? A good part of our lives are already gone, and we still have our mark to make. Excuse me, perhaps you've already made yours, but I haven't. Me, I've just begun and have a long way to go. It'll be dark soon, and we'll both be gone in the morning. Perhaps you'll stay hidden, raise a herd, and survive? I hope you do it, old fella. I really do."

Happy to have seen just one Wood Buffalo; in the morning, Sharp headed south. After weeks of traveling, he found himself back in Cheyenne. He walked inside a bar and eatery, and the crowd was rough. Finding a table, he sat down and ordered food. Hungry but aware that he was being watched, he ate, paid for his meal, and walked out. Followed by three tough men, Sharp went to his horse, alert to what might come next.

"Hold on thar, Mister," said the largest of the group.

The three men were alike in dress and manner, wearing ragged beards and dirty clothing.

"What can I do for you, gentleman?" asked Sharp, his hand resting on the handle of his Colt.

"Huh," said the leader. "Spread out, boys. He's makin' fun of us."

Before they could separate, and taking them by surprise, Sharp pulled his pistol and lay the barrel soundly on the heads of two of the men. Both fell.

"Whatever your intent," said Sharp to the bigger man, "you're not going to be getting anything of mine."

The would-be thief opened his mouth in a twisted snarl and exposed rotten teeth.

"Mister, I don't need no help to take care of you."

Sharp stepped into the street, still holding his pistol, and watched as the filthy man pulled a knife.

"A knife against a revolver? Not too bright, are you?"

The thief walked closer and lunged. Sharp hit the man's wrist with the barrel of his revolver, and the knife dropped to the ground. The aggressor grunted in pain, as Sharp struck once more on the side of the man's face, and the big fellow collapsed. In disgust, Sharp held his breath while he picked up the filthy creature and, with difficulty, slung him over his saddle. Taking reins, the winner of the altercation led his mount and the thief to the sheriff's office.

"What you got there, stranger?" asked the sheriff, coming out onto the boardwalk.

"This fellow and two others tried to rob me outside the bar and eatery up the street. Not too bright either. He attacked me with a knife while I held a pistol."

"What's your name, Mister?"

"Tom Sharp, and yours?"

"I'm Sheriff B. K. Boswell, and what you got there is Dirty Harry. Did you kill him?"

"Naw, he's just knocked cold. His partners are in the same condition up yonder."

"Are you the Tom Sharp that worked for the Railroad?"

"I am. Have you heard of me?" asked Sharp.

"Why man, in this country, everyone's heard of you. I'm short some men. How would you like to work for me?"

"Doing what?"

"Cleaning up the town and a whole territory of undesirables. We got a heap of 'em."

"What's the pay?"

"Fifty a month, plus fees. We got a lot of fees."

"How many deputies do you have?"

"Well, I got you and two others if you take the job. I warn you, it's a tough one."

"I figured that. I'll take it. What about those two thieves up the street?"

"Let's put this feller in lockup, and I'll get a horse, and we'll collect the other two. When we finish this, I have to cover jurisdiction back in Laramie. You'll stay here in Cheyenne with my other deputies."

***

For the latter year of 1867 and into 1868, Sharp wore a badge and became Deputy Sheriff of Cheyenne, Dakota Territory.

Having given a Cheyenne address, Sharp received his first letter from Mr. and Mrs. Durrett. It was short and to the point. In part, it read:

"Mister Sharp, write more or hurry your affairs and come marry our daughter. She isn't getting any younger. We are doing our best to hold the marriage pact together."

His response was longer. He told the parents in great detail about working for the railroad, hunting buffalo, and surviving an Indian attack. The last part of the letter was about being appointed a lawman in Cheyenne. He added, "Give my regards to Katherine."

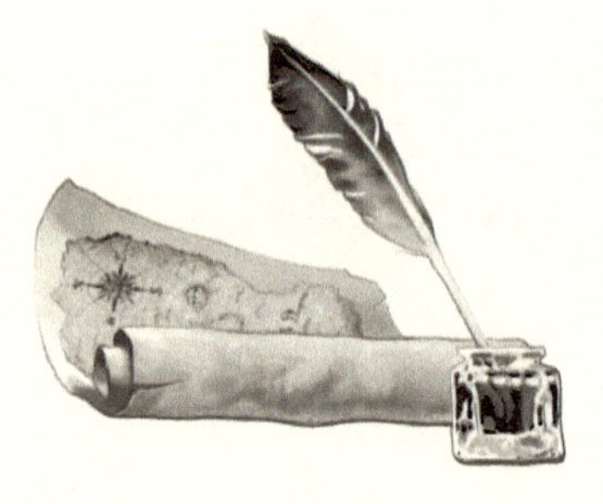

CHAPTER 10

Deputy Sharp would often eat breakfast at a local café. There he met John Williams and John White. They were honest, likable fellows, meat suppliers for the town restaurants. When Sharp was off duty, they met at a favorite bar in the evenings. They would drink beer, play cards, and talk half the night.

One evening, Williams began to share his thoughts of what he would like to do in the future.

"Me and White have kicked around half the west, doing one job after another," said Williams. "I'm not getting any younger, and I'm looking to settle down."

"You never said nothin' about that, partner," said White. "Not in all the time we were together. How's come you're talking about it now?"

"Tom sort of drags out a man's ambitions and puts them on the table," said Williams.

"What sort of settling you looking for?" asked Sharp.

"Well," began Williams, "I'd sure like to have a spread. Not expensive land, mind you, but purty land. Like in some valley with a river running through it. All protected like."

"John," said White, "now's you takin' my dreams and layin' 'em out."

"And you're going to do that with White?" asked Sharp.

"He'd look funny living in my cabin with my wife and kids."

"You going to dump me, partner!" exclaimed White. "After all the time we's together?"

"Didn't say that," said Williams. "Would favor it if you homesteaded right next to me, then you's and I could sort of look out for each other, like always."

"You think I could get a woman to marry me?" asked White, and then laughed, and the others joined in.

"I've been asking myself the same question," said Williams.

"I've sort of got a wife lined up," said Sharp, "but I don't dare go back to Missouri and get her until I've made my mark."

Eagerly, White and Williams asked about Sharp's woman. And the deputy sheriff merely stated that her name was Katherine, that she was fair beyond description, and that she was promised to him.

"Man, if I had a woman like that, I wouldn't make her wait," exclaimed White.

"Me either," added Williams. "Aren't you afraid of losing her?"

"I am, but I can't go back until I make my fortune."

"All right then, Sharp, if you say so," said Williams. "Now tell me, if we homesteaded on land, filed, and got the patent, what would you raise?"

"I know exactly," replied Sharp. "I'd start with horses. I'd mix thoroughbreds with mustangs and raise up good sound mounts. Then I'd have cattle and mix in better stock. Maybe send back east for some bulls. I might even start some kind of business."

"Whew, that sounds like a lot," said Williams.

"No pigs?" asked White.

"No," replied Sharp.

"Well, we can't settle here," said White. "It's got to be warmer winters away from the snow and cold."

"Agreed," said Williams.

"You don't think maybe the three of us could head south, maybe to Colorado Territory, and find a place?" asked White.

Over several months, the three men discussed their options and finally made plans to move south.

***

Tom Sharp left his badge and stint as deputy sheriff to join up with John Williams and John White. Sharp purchased ten mustangs, two of them stallions. White and Williams preferred to travel by prairie wagons. Together they headed eastward and down into Colorado. Most nights, they camped some distance from pioneers heading west along the California/Oregon Trail. Reaching Denver, they took the main road further south along the Front Range, looking for land to homestead. At Huerfano Peak, the men turned west and followed the Huerfano River. They stopped and rested at Badito, the county seat. It was on a rare water source, and there was a hotel, general store, and flour mill on the river. The three men ate their first good dinner in weeks at a small cantina.

"I've never seen you fellows before," commented the owner.

"We're lookin' for good ranch land," said Williams.

"We've come all the way down from what is now called Wyoming Territory," interjected White. "What we want is a protected place with water and warm winters."

"Land that we can homestead," added Sharp.

"If you don't mind the Indians, you might find what you are looking for further west. Follow the river and go past the place called Gardner. You'll be in the mountains, and there's some mighty fine valleys."

"Exactly what kind of Indians are you talking about?" asked Williams.

"Well," explained the cantina owner, "there's the Utes; they're friendly; it's a different story with the Apache and Arapaho."

"Do the settlers around here get attacked very often?" asked Sharp.

"Now that you mention it, not so much recently."

"Thanks for the advice," said Sharp. "Soon as we finish lunch and buy supplies, we'll try to find that land you were talking about."

Resupplying, they headed west. Miles from Badito, they came under attack. Apache arrows struck the two wagons, and the line of tied mustangs reared up and escaped. The horses scattered across the prairie as more Indians appeared. Warriors with rifles began firing, Williams and White slapped reins, and their four-horse rigs and wagons raced across the open land. Sharp, not willing to lose his mustangs, chased after them. Pistol in hand, he began firing back at the Apaches.

Sharp found himself far from the racing wagons and his friends. A small band of Apaches had splintered off. They were headed straight for him. Sharp pulled his horse up to a rocky outcropping and dismounted. He grabbed his Henry, climbed up, and used a large boulder for cover. The mounted warriors advanced, and with each shot, an Indian pony lost a rider. The accuracy of Sharp's rifle caused the remaining Apaches to turn and start back to join their fellows chasing the wagons.

Sharp reloaded his Henry, and then he saw a different band of Indians gallop out of the low ground. Holding rifles and bows, the second band of warriors shot at the attacking Apaches. Through the confusion of dust and noise, the two wagons rode out of danger. Just as quickly as it started, it ended. The Apaches disappeared off the plain as if they were never there, except for the dead they left behind.

A lone warrior appeared his manner and dress that of a chief. Tom Sharp reached his mustang and mounted. Holding up his right arm and hand, the Indian rode forward.

"Plenty shooting and plenty dead," said the chief. "You are safe now. Apaches, no good."

"Thank you," said Sharp. "Who are you?"

"Your people call us Utes. I am Chief Ouray. And you?"

"I am Tom Sharp, and those men on the wagons are John Williams and John White."

"You are lucky fellows," smiled the chief. "Lucky we were hunting game. Come, we ride to the wagons. My warriors gather your horses. You come to my camp. We talk, we eat, and maybe make trade."

Chief Ouray and his band led the three travelers into the Huerfano River Valley. It was a stretch of land between many vast mountain peaks, including the Greenhorn, Sheep, and Silver Mountains. Coming down from the Sangre de Cristo Mountains, the Huerfano River fed the lush valley with water. When the three men drove their horses and wagons onto the green plain, they were amazed and awe-struck by its magnificence.

They spent a day and night in the Ute encampment, and to show gratitude for their rescue, Sharp traded two of his mares for hides and dried meat.

"You make a good trade," said Chief Ouray. "You live here now? A place with plenty of water."

"We might," said Sharp. "It looks promising."

"To keep the peace, I signed a treaty. Your government took this land."

"Sorry to hear that, chief."

"Better Utes live than have war. Some of my people don't agree. Too many soldiers, and they have too many guns."

"I suppose…," responded Sharp.

"We friends now?" asked Chief Ouray. "Perhaps you visit? Always we fight the Apaches and Arapaho. When we are here, we make the whites safe from bad Indians. Maybe when you are settled, we make more trade?"

"Sounds right to me, chief," replied Sharp. "Give us more time to decide."

The three men took charge of their gear and rode out of the Indian camp.

***

Riding further into the valley, they met up with an old timer. He was on a spirited horse and, despite his age, rode erect like a military man.

"Gutentag!" greeted the oldster.

With a sweep of his hand and in a most formal manner, he indicated the valley, the river, and the mountains.

"It ist magnificent, ist it not?"

Williams and White climbed down off their wagons and stood next to Sharp and his horse.

"It is," the men agreed.

"I'm Captain Charles Deus."

"Hello, Captain," exclaimed Williams. "I'm John, this here is my pard John White, and the fellow on the horse is the famous Tom Sharp."

"Famous?" asked the captain.

"At least in Californy and the Dakota Territory," explained Williams.

"My friend exaggerates," commented Sharp. "There's no doubt about it. This is a mighty fine valley. Do you live here?"

"Been here since '58. I commanded a cavalry unit in Mexico. After the conflict, I came north und started a ranch. Vhere do you come from?" asked the captain.

"Sharp was a deputy sheriff in Cheyenne, and Williams and I were meat suppliers," explained White. "We came down here lookin' for land with water and mild winters."

"This is a good place. There is land here to homestead. I vill show you."

"You don't know us, sir," said Sharp."

"My business vas commanding men," replied Captain Deus, and he smiled. "I know good fellows vhen I see them!"

Captain Deus did as promised. Each section of land bordered the Huerfano River.

"I know dis country," said Captain Deus, "you vill not find better homestead than this. Do vhat I did, each of you file on a hundred and sixty acres, and the land is yours."

The three men nodded their heads. There was no doubt they had found the land they had spent so many months searching for. The next day they rode to Badito and filled out paperwork to homestead their quarter sections.

CHAPTER 11

"Not that I don't trust the captain, but I asked around," said Williams. "I'm told the Huerfano River coming down from the mountains, never goes dry."

"Folks I talked to say the same," said White.

"We're lucky to find this valley," exclaimed Sharp.

"Tom," said Williams. "We've been thinkin' on this for months. Now that we're here, how do we get started?"

"I met up with the captain at the store in Gardner. He invited us for dinner at his place. Wants us to meet his family. Says he has a Spanish wife and two sons."

"When is that?" asked Williams.

"Tomorrow."

"I'm glad he's willing to help us," said White.

"Yeah," laughed Williams. "I like that old German."

***

"They went to the captain's home, and it was a large wooden framed building. Deus saw them coming. From the porch, he pointed to a hitching rail. The three guests dismounted and tied reins.

"Come in, come in. My wife has dinner ready."

Sharp, Williams, and White followed their host into the house. He led them to the dining room and a long table.

"Gentleman," said the German, "meet my family. My vife, Juanita. The tall boy ist Frank, and the shorter one Pete."

Mrs. Deus pointed to chairs, and they all sat down.

"A fine house, sir," said White.

"Ve only have one life," laughed the captain. "This land has been goot to me."

A young Spanish girl brought in steaming dishes and placed them on a cart. She went around the table and ladled out the food.

"Ve'll eat first," said Deus, and he laughed again. "Best to appease the hunger and then talk."

They had glasses of wine with their meal. Captain Deus commanded the conversation. There were polite responses from the guests, and little else was said. After dinner, the table was cleared by the serving girl. With a nod from the captain, Juanita and the boys disappeared.

"Now ve can talk."

"Your cattle business must be going very well," interjected Williams.

"It ist. But that is not all that built this place. When I first got here, I discovered some gold and quite a bit of silver. Hence, vhat you see."

"You live very well," said White.

"Vell enough," answered Deus. "Someday, I believe the three of you may have similar advantages."

"Wouldn't that be something!" exclaimed White.

Mrs. Deus brought a tray with glasses and a pitcher of cold beer.

"I brew my own and keep it in the ice house. I like cold beer."

"Who doesn't?" laughed White.

"So," said Deus. "I have been thinking vhat advice I can give you."

The three men nodded their heads. The captain spoke for some time.

"I haf talked too long," laughed the rancher. "My vife, she complains, I can talk a man's ears off. You haf questions?"

"It sounds like you can help us start our ranches," said Williams.

"I vill try," said the captain.

"First, we register our brand at the county seat in Badito?" asked White.

"And after that, you'll bring workers?" added Williams.

"Yes," said Deus, nodding his head.

"I'm confused; you want us to build for the animals first?" asked Sharp.

"Like I did vhen I first got here. You need corrals, a stable, and a barn. Then, you can build cabins for the vinter."

"And you will sell us cattle?" asked White.

"I sell them cheap. And once you brand, you run them vith mine on grass in the high country. In vinter, you bring them down to your ranches."

"Is this how you raise your herd?" asked Sharp.

"Yes," replied Deus. "My men have cabins up there. This is open range, and there are no fences.

Cattle must be watched closely. Vee must protect our herds from the catamounts, varmints, and those who steal."

"Do you have much rustling?" asked Sharp.

"Sometimes," replied Deus. "But ve do not tolerate such. Ve take care of the problem."

"Sir, we appreciate your help," said Sharp.

"Tut, tut, say no more. I am thinking, I vant good neighbors. This is still vild country."

Deus finished his beer, repressed a yawn, smiled, and stood up. The guests did the same. He led them to the foyer.

"Captain," said Sharp. "When we register our brands, I'll send word. We look forward to meeting your workers."

"Goot, I vill have them ready."

Going to their horses, the men mounted and rode towards Sharp's homestead, where they kept their wagons and supplies. For once, they hardly said anything.

"Man! What would we do without that German?" asked Williams.

The three of them worked hard to put up a fenced enclosure for their animals. For the next few weeks, they slept under canvas. Having flipped coins, Sharp won, and the building would begin on his ranch.

***

Deus sold ten head each to Williams and White; Sharp purchased twenty. If they wanted more, they would have to buy them elsewhere. It took less than a week to brand the cattle. It was only accomplished by using the old man's corrals. Together the four of them drove the cattle up onto mountain grass to be guarded by Deus's workers.

Labor on the three ranches was cheap, and the work went quickly. Once the horses were sheltered, cabins were completed. Hay was cut and stored in barns and under shelters. In the fall, they drove their herds off the high range and down into the Huerfano Valley. They brought in calves, separated them, and each got their mother's brand.

The winters in the valley were mild. Occasionally there blew in northeasters. The temperature dropped and sometimes deposited large amounts of snow, but within a week, the temperatures rose to the forties, fifties, and sixties, and the snow evaporated into the dry air, a peculiarity to the arid conditions on the high mountain desert.

In Gardner, prices were high, and often there was a scarcity of merchandise. Tom Sharp took it upon himself to find a driver to ship goods from Pueblo for himself and his two friends. Year around, a steady stream of wagons and riders passed his ranch on the way to Taos. Travelers stopped in Gardner and attempted to buy supplies. Often, they went without. After a year of this, Sharp got the idea of having a trading post on his ranch. Near the trail, in a thicket of cottonwoods, he built a large adobe building. He called it Buzzard Roost after the buzzards that perched in the trees. Immediate trade in supplies began with travelers and with Ute Indians. Sharp expanded the structure and moved into more luxurious quarters.

***

Once again, Sharp wrote to Mr. and Mrs. Durrett. In the letter, he told them he was very close to being able to provide Katherine a comfortable life. He described settling in the Huerfano River Valley, homesteading a ranch, raising cattle and horses, and building a trading post.

On his own, Sharp explored the land further. He spent time panning for gold along the Huerfano

River and Pass Creek. Flakes were found, but nothing of significance. When he found copper mixed with other minerals, he believed it to be of sufficient quantity to mine. Visiting Captain Deus, they discussed the possibilities. Deus suggested they build a stamping mill on his homestead and become partners.

After the stamping mill was running, Sharp purchased one hundred and sixty acres a mile from his trading post. In 1870, he laid out a town he called Malachite for the malachite copper he found. Workman came, built cabins, and some labored in the stamping mill while others mined copper.

Tom Sharp was now earning money. Trading for hides with the Utes, he hit upon buying Union and British surplus officer uniforms. The Utes and some of the Spanish liked the blue uniforms with fancy epaulets and brass buttons. Making money hand over fist, Sharp began to look for a manager to run his Trading Post and other affairs. It was getting close to the time to go to Missouri and meet his bride. Still, he wanted to reinforce his businesses before leaving.

It would be at least another decade before the railroad would arrive. Often Sharp traveled to Pueblo with a huge freight wagon to gather supplies. He took his new man Pedro, and together they loaded the wagon with trade goods and headed back to Buzzard Roost. On the return trip, they encountered a disheveled fellow sitting alongside the road. Sharp, riding one of his fast mustangs, had the driver of the wagon stop.

"Stranger," said Sharp, "you look to be in some distress."

"My horse, my rifle, my saddlebags, my food, and my canteen ran away this morning. The darn thing threw me, and I think my leg's busted."

Dismounting, Sharp motioned to Pedro to get down. Together, they picked up the prostrate fellow. He screamed bloody murder. They laid him in the shadow of a large rock. Seeing the right leg was twisted, the two men gathered splints and rope. The Spanish driver quickly set the bone, and he and Sharp secured the leg.

"That hurt," said the stranger, sitting up against a boulder.

"Si, señor, I fix many broken bones," said the driver. "Pedro tell you now. Make crutches. Don't walk six weeks. You lucky fellow to find me."

"What's your name?" asked Sharp to the man sitting in the dirt.

"George Elmire," answered the fellow. "No use to fix me up. Something else bad will happen like it always does. You might as well shoot me now and get it over with. I'd do it myself if I had a pistol or rifle. I've been thinking about it for some time now. It is all ordained. Falling off my horse was the final bit of bad luck I'm going to take."

"Don't talk like that," said Sharp. "We found you, didn't we? We fixed your leg. Now how about a drink of water and some jerky?"

Pedro rushed to bring a water jug and a pouch containing jerky. He handed the items one at a time to the injured man. Despite Pedro's protestations, George Elmire gulped the water. Then he set the jug close to him and began chewing.

"I must admit, that was extremely good refreshment," said George. "May I inquire your name, sir?"

"I'm Tom Sharp. I own a spread and a store about thirty miles from here. We'll get you up on the wagon, and I'll take you to my place."

"Very solicitous of you, sir," said George.

"Que?" asked Pedro.

“I think he means we are being considerate.”

“Yes, very astute,” retorted George.

“You are an educated man?” asked Sharp.

“Back east, I attended a university or two,” replied George. “I was a professor, but I found it stifling and quit. Then looking for excitement, I headed west. Each step I have taken since has been a steady decline.”

“Well, cheer up, George Elmire,” said his rescuer. “I have been looking for an educated man to look after my affairs. Suppose we get you up on the wagon. I’ll tie my horse and climb aboard with you, and we’ll talk. Let’s see how it goes.”

“Much obliged, kind sir. You and Pedro may be my salvation. Just when I thought God and the universe turned on me.”

Pedro crossed himself at the mention of God.

George was a diminutive man weighing around a hundred pounds. Getting him up and into the wagon seat didn’t take a lot of effort. George complained of pain, but they managed to make him and his injured leg as comfortable as possible. Pedro, doing a kindness, found his bottle of mescal. He had a cup and poured it half full.

“Señor George, I do a favor. For the pain.”

George sniffed the alcohol and then, shrugging his shoulders, swallowed it down.

"Gracias," said George.

"De nada," replied Pedro.

"Muy amable de su parte, mi amable señor," said George.

"You speak Spanish?" asked Tom Sharp.

"I do, although I am told my accent is terrible. And I can speak, read, and write in Latin and Greek, the so-called dead languages."

"Can you keep accounting books, tally up figures, make a running account of supplies?" asked Sharp.

"My good man," replied George, "if the remuneration were sufficient, I suppose I could manage."

"Sir?"

"Money! Pay! Although I must say, given my circumstances, I don't expect much. I would think food, a room, care and companionship would be sufficient for the present."

"Done," replied Sharp. "I will give you, say, several weeks. I can hire an Indian girl to take care of cooking and washing clothes for you. I assume you would be well enough to go over the books sitting up. You don't have to walk to be able to do that."

George Elmire laughed.

"I suppose not."

"I warn you," said Sharp. "I run a busy trading post. My clientele is varied. Ute Indians usually trade with hides for clothing and supplies. Then there are travelers on the way to Taos, both white and Spanish."

"I see. I'm not afraid of work."

"I also have cattle and horses for sale. And, a mile from my trading post, a partner and I have a copper stamping mill. Like I said, I have been looking for an educated man."

"I believe, sir, that taking care of your accounts will be far less taxing than my prior occupations."

It was fortuitous that Sharp met George Elmire. The man not only took to maintaining accounts but demanded professional ledgers to keep a proper inventory of goods and items sold and acquired.

With George Elmire handling much of the business, Sharp became more involved in breeding his horses. A surprising development was the Utes betting on horse races along the road to Buzzard Roost. Chief Ouray would often accompany his band and take part. Eventually, Sharp became involved in the impromptu races, betting one of his mixed thoroughbreds against an Indian pony.

It wasn't long before the trading post became the site of frequent horse races between whites and Indians. This built up to a big race between an Indian horse and a thoroughbred owned by a rancher near Taos. The day before the race, misfortune struck Chief Ouray's tribe. The Utes lost a fight with the Arapahos. They buried their dead and cared for their wounded. Their dispositions were demoralized, and the southern Ute tribe was in a gruesome mood.

This did not stop the scheduled race. White gamblers came from as far as Pueblo and Taos. The thoroughbred from the Clifton Ranch at Red River Crossing in New Mexico Territory was brought to the Buzzard Roost Trading Post. The group was made of westerners, Tom Hoggs, A. G. Thornhill, George Thompson, and Thike Stockton. Other horse betters arrived from surrounding ranches. The tribe of Uncompahgre Utes from Ouray's band arrived. The betting increased. A judge was to be selected, and Chief Ouray made his choice.

"I want Sharpy for our judge," said the chief.

The whites were pleased and surprised as they thought an Indian would be chosen. The white betters, in favor of the New Mexico racehorse, picked Baldy Scott as their judge. The large crowd became more excited, and the betting increased. Blankets were placed in Indian fashion on the ground, and silver, gold, and paper money were laid down. An Indian kid in breechclout rode the Ute horse. A little fellow named Betts had the New Mexico racer, and Baldy Scott, the judge for the whites set the two steeds off. The race was close, neck and neck, Bett's flogged his horse mercilessly, but in the end, the Indian pony won by a head.

Angry whites clamored to Tom Sharp.

"Tied race! Tied race!" yelled the whites.

Baldy Scott, too afraid to judge, said nothing.

Sharp stood his ground as Chief Ouray, his Indians, and the whites became silent to hear his verdict.

"It's the Indian's race," exclaimed the post trader.

Boo's and hisses were followed by crestfallen comments. Resentment against the Indians by the whites remained high. The chief of the band signaled for his warriors to fold the blankets with the thousands of dollars they just won. Tom Sharp did a brave thing siding with the Indians, and from that moment on, the trust between the Indian Chief, his band, and the white trader increased.

***

Tom Sharp was now a rich man. The epic moment had arrived, and it was finally time to meet his promised wife, Katherine. He informed his friends, White and Williams, that he was leaving. He told them he had men securing his properties and possessions, but if George Elmire ran into trouble, he would ask for help. Williams and White agreed. Confident his businesses were well cared for, he prepared for his trip back to his birthplace, Marion County, Missouri.

CHAPTER 12

Tom Sharp wrote that he was coming and the date of his arrival. He was now thirty-two years of age. Katherine Durrett was twenty-six. She was an old maid but kept that way by her own choice and that of her parents. All these years, she had been waiting for the man she promised to marry. During that time, all she had were the letters from Tom Sharp.

This meeting will determine my future, thought Sharp. *When I left, she was only seventeen, youthful, and full of admiration for my Southern uniform. In truth, we barely knew each other. Will the girl be so enthusiastic after all this time?*

Throughout his life, Tom Sharp had been afraid of nothing until now. The entire train ride was one of complete apprehension and anxiety.

***

Receiving his letter, Katherine waited for the man she had agreed to marry. Once again, she pored over the messages, imagined his exploits, and filled in the details his communications neglected. In the last year, she became exceedingly impatient and resentful. So, when Tom Sharp knocked on the door of the Durrett home, the sight of the slim, bearded man did not impress her as it once may have. Greeting the three Durretts at the door, Tom, dressed in an expensive new suit, a fresh haircut, and a trimmed beard, entered their home. He smelled of the sweet hair tonic the barber had applied that morning.

"Mr. Durrett," began the suitor. "Sir, I am Tom Sharp, and I am here to seek the hand of your daughter, Katherine."

"Welcome," said the father, "Mr. Sharp, we've been waiting a very long time. Daughter, I present your suitor, Mister William Thomas Sharp!"

Smiling, Tom attempted to hand Katherine a bouquet of flowers. She made no effort to take them, and it was her mother who took the flowers from the hands of the younger man.

Chapter 12

"Mighty pleased to see you, Miss Katherine," said Tom. "I know nine years have passed, but you are still as pretty as the day I left. Prettier, if I may say so."

"What you mean, Tom Sharp, is that I am more mature. Nine years is entirely too long. Your letters hardly suffice."

"Katherine!" exclaimed her parents. "Mind your manners!"

"Well, sir?" asked the younger woman.

Tom Sharp laughed and then, in a spontaneous loss of decorum, grabbed Katherine by the shoulders and soundly kissed her on the lips. The parents gasped, and Katherine stood mesmerized. Tom kissed her again, this time longer and harder. And then, prepared for anything, he backed up.

"Now, Miss Katherine," said Tom, smiling, "does that prove my ardor? I will be happy to explain what I did all those years. And there wasn't one moment I did not think of you. I would have written to you directly, but your parents forbade it. I assure you, Katherine, I come here to offer you my fortune and my future. That is if you will have me."

Katherine, for the first time in her life, stood speechless. Finally, she overcame the most passionate kiss any man had ever given her.

"Well, sir!" she retorted. "You take advantage! I am not merchandise to be bought and sold. For years I have waited, and now I am thinking how foolish I was. Your years of neglect can hardly be endured."

To the young woman's surprise, Tom Sharp laughed again. There was a stubborn streak to Katherine Durrett, and his response angered her beyond measure.

"It will take much more than flowers, an inappropriate kiss, and words to win my heart, Tom Sharp," said Katherine Durrett. "Your manners, sir, can hardly be tolerated!"

With that statement, the disturbed woman turned and walked out the front door, slamming it behind her. In obvious anger, she stepped forward onto the front porch and stood holding the white wooden railing.

"We didn't expect that from her," said Mr. Durrett.

"Katherine has always been headstrong," said the mother. "I'm afraid your letters and our support were not enough to fill her heart. Perhaps we were wrong in not permitting you to correspond directly with her. Lately, she has been rude and restless."

"Does she have another suitor?" asked Sharp.

"Of course not!" began her father.

"To be honest, Mr. Sharp," replied the mother, "she has a very active social life. She is an adult."

"Perhaps I arrived just in time. Where does Katherine spend most of her days?"

"Church," the Durretts replied.

"She is very involved in fund-raising," said the mother.

"I have been remiss," said Sharp. "It is difficult to ask any woman to wait so many years."

"Well, just don't stand there!" exclaimed Mister Durrett. "Get out there and court my daughter. She's waited this long. Man, break through that shell!"

With determination on his face, Tom opened the door and walked out.

"Miss Katherine," he said. "I apologize for my abruptness. I can see how time has worked against us. And, my letters were sparse."

"Sparse?" exclaimed Katherine. "That is the word you use? Sir, you and my parents assume too much."

"Do you have other suitors, Katherine?"

"To be honest, I have several. I haven't been living in a vacuum."

"Then why haven't you married?"

"I've often wondered that myself," replied Katherine. "It certainly wasn't because of lack of offers."

"Could it be you still care for me?"

"Perhaps it was the promise I made. But seeing you here today after all these years, and how you act…well…I am NOT your possession!"

"Then I will make it right," said Tom. "No matter how long it takes, no matter who else stands before me, I will show you I care more. It was the vision of you, our marriage, and having children that kept me going. I have worked toward that vision all this time."

"Words, sir!" replied Katherine. "They seem to come easily to you."

"That is because, in this, I have spent years rehearsing what I would say when we met. I have told no other living soul of these dreams."

"I bet you have spoken about me to others. Of the sheltered girl who pines for a man she doesn't even know."

"I have spoken of you one time to three friends. Tersely and only that we were promised."

"Why, sir, did you not say such things in your letters?"

"Because your parents forbid such familiarity."

"Well, they were wrong."

"I see you are very angry. Could I invite you to supper? Could we go for a walk? Or just sit and talk?"

"Not today, Mister Sharp. I am too upset to succumb to any notion of entertaining you!"

"Then tomorrow. I will bring pictures of the valley, of the trading post, and the river that runs nearby. You will see the home I offer you. I need you to complete my life. Everything I have done, everything I have accomplished, every dollar I have earned is for us."

Katherine did not answer, and reaching out, Tom lightly touched her hand. Then he went down the steps, onto the walk, and towards his hotel. Sharp walked swiftly, stiffly erect, and he looked exactly like what he was, a westerner, his face burned deep brown by the sun. The young woman stood and watched him. It did help his cause that he looked much more dashing than those other men who pursued her.

It took great effort on Tom Sharp's part to gain the consent of this beautiful, mature woman. Like everything he did in his life, he gave it his all. They attended church activities, dined at restaurants, and went to dances. Sharp courted with fervor and filled her house with cut flowers. He sent her poems written by famous writers and notes filled with words of devotion.

But it was Sharp's drive to leave no stone unturned in winning the affection of the woman he hoped to marry that he took the scholarly advice from the librarian in town. Under the learned man's guidance, Tom sat down and read Shakespeare's sonnets. It was number 116 that he finally selected. It was this poem that finally won Katherine's heart. He had it specially printed and placed in a decorated envelope.

SONNET 116
Let me not to the marriage of true minds
Admit impediments. Love is not love
Which alters when it alteration finds,
Or bends with the remover to remove:
O no! It is an ever-fixed mark
That looks on tempests and is never shaken;
It is the star to every wandering bark,
Whose worth's unknown, although his height be taken

Love's not Time's fool, though rosy lips and cheeks
Within his bending sickle's compass come:
Love alters not with his brief hours and weeks,
But bears it out even to the edge of doom.
If this be error and upon me proved,
I never writ, nor no man ever loved.
William Shakespeare

After delivery of the printed missive, Tom Sharp went out and purchased a new suit, obtained a haircut, and a tightly trimmed beard. He arrived at the Durrett home in a rented buggy. Smelling sweetly of hair tonic, a large bouquet of red roses in hand, the suitor knocked on Katherine Durrett's door. He was smiling, enthusiastic, and full of high hopes. After all, Katherine was a beauty and, thanks to her parents, a well-educated and charming young lady. A spectacular prize of femininity for any man in this world.

That evening there was a church social. It began with a formal dinner presided over by the minister. The congregation brought dishes, and the main course was prepared and cooked outside throughout the day. It was quarters of a roasted cow. This was cooked, cut, and served by the young teens of the church. The dinner was held in the basement of the parish hall, a separate building adjacent to the church. The adults wore their Sunday best, and people enthusiastically greeted each other. The minister asked a blessing, and the dinner began.

After the meal, the tables were cleared, and parishioners climbed stairs to the main hall, a large open room. At one end was a stage, and upon it sat musicians who began to play a waltz. Quickly couples went to the floor and started dancing.

"Miss Katherine," said Tom Sharp, bowing and reaching out a hand, "would you be so kind as to allow me the pleasure?"

Katherine smiled and extended her gloved hand, and together they joined the dancing couples swirling around the floor. Tom was careful to be formal and polite, cognizant of his best manners. He was observant, and when his date looked like she needed respite from the dance floor, he took her hand and led her to a bench along the side of the room, where others were sitting, temporarily catching their breath.

The suitor was as solicitous as he could be, and twice he excused himself to go and collect the cake and punch refreshment provided. And twice he took away the dishes and cups to return to dancing. Later in the evening, having thoroughly enjoyed the music, the dancing, and the colorful crowd, Mister Sharp formally broached the subject of taking a buggy ride. Katherine nodded in the affirmative over the noise of the music. The suitor went off in search of her wrap and returned with it. Helping her he then led her outside. The evening was cool.

Tom left Katherine at the door and went alone to the church lot. He retrieved his rented buggy and drove to pick her up. Getting down, careful of her long dress, the man helped Katherine step up into the conveyance. Tom had the foresight to bring a blanket from the hotel. He gathered it and helped to cover the young lady from the coolness of the evening. Boarding, Sharp slapped reins, and the horse pulled the buggy forward onto the street. Hooves clopped loudly on the hard brick pavement; the young woman slid closer. She smiled and, in accommodation, shared part of the blanket.

Tom began to speak, thought better of it, and waited. Finally, it was Katherine who spoke first.

"Thomas," began Katherine, "I was very surprised and delighted to get that decorative card."

"You mean the poem?" asked Tom Sharp.

"Yes. I wouldn't expect you to know about Shakespeare's Sonnets, how…"

"As you know, the schools here in Marion County are excellent, and I finished the eighth grade. And, through the years, many books have come to my hands. But the Sonnets I did not know."

"Then how…did you send me that particular one?"

"In this, I admit my education is limited. I asked for help. I went to the librarian for advice, and he gave me the Sonnets to read. I read them all, and it was number 116 that I picked out for you."

"And my parents never told you how much I love Shakespeare and…"

"No, that they did not tell me. But if they had thought of it…"

"And you are telling the truth?"

"I am."

"Well, Mister Thomas Sharp, in school, we happened to study Shakespeare and this particular sonnet. We analyzed its meaning, forward and backward, and it has become my favorite. You are very fortunate, wise, or lucky indeed to capture my attention in this manner."

"Then you liked it?"

"Thomas, I shall keep your card in a special place for the rest of my life."

Deliberately, Tom had steered the horse down secluded streets and away from the gas lights. Now on a dark road, the suitor pulled leather, stopped the buggy, and tied the reins off.

"Does that mean there is hope for me, Katherine? That finally I have reached your heart?"

Instead of answering, Katherine slid closer to the man she had been promised to for nine years. She reached out and put a hand on his chest. Sliding his right arm around her shoulder, Tom pulled Katherine towards him. Leaning closer, he kissed her gently and lightly on the lips. It was she who pressed harder against his mouth, and in great ardor, their lips parted, and they kissed passionately. This went on for some time, and feeling the heat of each other's bodies beneath the blanket, it was Tom who finally pushed away.

"You are magnificent, Katherine. So beautiful, so bright, and intelligent. So full of grace and passion about everything around you. You are everything I have ever hoped for. I do love you so."

"Yes, but sir, you push me away?"

"If I didn't, I may not have been able to stop. I am a grown man full of passion as well. I ask you now, formally, Katherine Durrett, I love you. Will you marry me?" '

"Before I answer, you must promise me one thing."

"Yes?"

"I am an only child, and unlike other young ladies, I have grown up with a certain amount of independence. Regarding really important decisions, you must promise me, should we marry, that you will give me deference and equal say."

"And if I said it was a man's place to..."

"I would rather stay single than marry such a man."

"Then Katherine, you have my promise that when it comes to important decisions, we shall decide together."

"Then, Tom Sharp," replied Katherine, "I will marry you."

"Thank you, Katherine. You will not regret this."

In the dark, under the blanket, he moved closer to his future bride, and for an hour, they shared mutual passion.

***

Finally, after three months of courting, they were married. The Durretts spared no expense. The church wedding contained nearly the entire congregation, and the reception, half the county. The year was 1871. Immediately, Katherine informed her husband she would not live like a barbarian and began picking out furniture for their home at Buzzard Roost Ranch. Tom took the time to gather a railroad carload of thoroughbreds. He spent thousands, the best being a Kentucky racehorse named John White.

Railroad construction was advancing rapidly now that the War Between the States had ended. They could travel over the Transcontinental and made good time on the spur to Denver. There they hired men to haul a freight wagon with furniture and domestic supplies and to also herd the horses down along the Front Range. Stopping at various hotels for the convenience of Katherine, they took eleven days to reach the ranch. Excited, she directed George Elmire and his helpers to move the old furniture to the spare cabin where the accountant would live. Katherine directed the arrangement of the new furniture.

Sharp had the thoroughbreds placed in the stables and separated by corrals from the mustangs and Indian ponies. He explained his plans for breeding a strong riding horse with endurance and speed to his hired men.

Once settled, Katherine involved herself in all aspects of her husband's businesses. She also went out of her way to meet members of the growing community. Their life together seemed to go well. Katherine was allowed to have a say in most matters. Both planned and looked forward to eventually having a family.

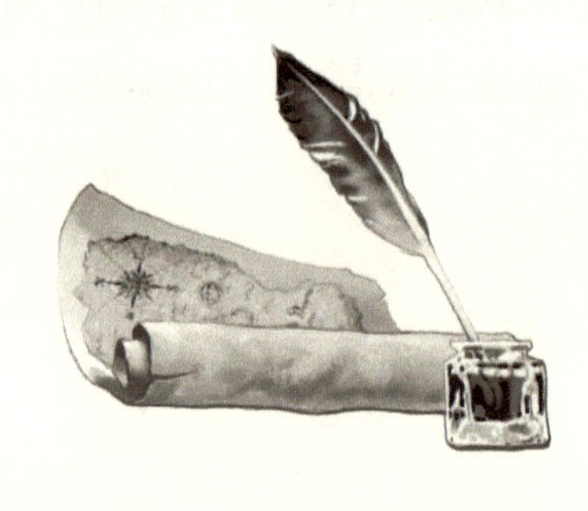

CHAPTER 13

In Malachite lived a community of white miners attempting to live off the harsh land. The men worked in the stamping mill or dug for copper. Susan Pepper, one of the more unfortunate and impoverished settlers, just had a baby. She was weak and ill, and so was her child. The father, Big Jack Pepper, was off on some drunk. There wasn't any food, water, or wood for the stone hearth. It was the week before Christmas, and there was only the celebration of birth and the miracle that two deprived humans still lived. Resting deep in the straw mattress bed and covered with several wool blankets, the mother lay on a pillow, her infant son barely able to suck what little milk she had. The West was harsh, and the Pepper family had it worse than most due to a derelict father.

Katherine Sharp was a concerned neighbor. Knowing the special circumstances, she knocked on the cabin door, and no one answered. Raising the latch, Mrs. Sharp called out.

"Sue? Sue Pepper, are you all right? It's Katherine Sharp."

There was a faint call, barely heard. Katherine entered, closed the door against a brisk cold wind, and ensured the latch caught. It was almost as cold inside as outside. Wind rustled through the cracks in the board walls. The visitor rushed to the bedroom and found the mother and child.

"Oh, Sue," said Katherine, "I thought I asked you to tell me…"

"I couldn't," whispered Sue Pepper.

The cold air in the small bedroom smelled. The mattress, without a sheet, was soiled with blood and human waste. Pulling a dirty blanket back, Katherine looked at the tiny infant. She saw, by some miracle, it was alive and suckling. Its umbilical cord still attached to the afterbirth lying somewhere in the bed. Ascertaining the circumstances and feeling great remorse for not checking on her neighbor sooner, the visitor spoke to the unfortunate woman.

"Sue," said Katherine, "I will be back. You and the baby stay covered and warm."

Rushing through the cold cabin, the concerned neighbor noticed no wood for the hearth and no water in the bucket. *You can bet there's not an ounce of food,* thought Katherine. *How could a man treat his wife in this manner? And those old bruises on Sue's face! How could a husband be so mean and cruel? If I don't get help, that woman and child will certainly die.*

Speeding down County Road 550, she came to Buzzard Roost Ranch. Katherine boarded her buggy, slapped reins harshly, and called for her blooded horse to jump into a run. Katherine barely stopped the conveyance before jumping to the ground, tying off reins, and rushing into the post.

"Tom! Tom, where are you!" shouted Katherine.

Behind the counter arranging ammunition, her husband rose up, startled by his wife's insistence.

"What's the matter with you, woman?" demanded Tom, "What are you all het up about?"

As briefly as she could, Katherine explained the situation.

"Well, there's no way around it," said Sharp, "until she gets better, she and the baby will have to come here to stay."

"Oh, husband, I was hoping you would say that."

"That man of hers isn't worth the powder to blow him away," said Sharp. "Do you think she can stand the trip in a wagon?"

"I don't know. She and the baby appear really weak. And...well...how can I put it? They're filthy, and they smell."

"You go get the midwife and bring her here. I'll find men, take the freight wagon, and pick up the woman and baby."

"Tom," said Katherine. "I think it should be the other way around. I'll go with George Elmire. He's like family. I should be there. Some delicate things need to be taken care of. Sue and the baby need to be washed and clothed first. I'll have to cut and tie off the baby's cord."

"Lordy, Lord, Katherine, what are you getting yourself into? Well, go ahead and grab what you need. I'll make sure the freight wagon is harnessed and ready before you go. Too bad we don't have a doctor around these parts."

Katherine Sharp was not sure the baby and Susan Pepper could stand the wagon ride to the trading post. The trader's wife brought a fresh nightgown, blankets, and cloth diapers for the infant. She entered the shack prepared to act.

Cutting the umbilical cord, Katherine set it aside. She had George fetch and boil water, and when ready, she washed the child and mother and then dressed them. They carried the infant and parent to the wagon, placed them on warm bedding, and covered them with blankets. On the way, Katherine tried to get the mother to drink the warm soup she had the foresight to bring.

Outside the trading post was a gathering of Ute Indians, and there were as many inside. The big freight wagon had to negotiate a path through them to the back of the building. Susan Pepper and her child were carried inside to one of the spare bedrooms. Throughout the day and until evening, Katherine fussed over her two patients. The midwife never came; she was too busy delivering babies. It wasn't until the next day that the skilled woman arrived.

"I'm Mrs. Sheppard," said the midwife. "I'm sorry I couldn't come when asked, but I delivered three Spanish babies yesterday; each one was some distance from the other."

The midwife was escorted into the bedroom. She examined the baby first and worked on properly cutting and disposing of the remainder of the umbilical cord. Then she examined the mother. In the kitchen, over coffee, Mrs. Sharp and Mrs. Sheppard discussed the situation.

"The baby is healthy but weak," said the midwife. "The mother's milk is drying up, and you will need a wet nurse. I know of a Ute woman who is strong and healthy who could come. Her name is Raine. She recently lost her husband and works for the white women in Malachite, doing laundry. Will you let her stay here? You would have to pay her. It wouldn't be much."

"Yes, I can do that," replied Katherine, "Is there anything else?"

"The mother is weak. It looks like she hasn't had decent food for a long time. The baby tore her up some, but that will heal. Her name is Susan Pepper?"

"Yes."

"I recommend you keep her confined to bed and feed her soup. It will be touch and go if she makes it. That woman is nearly starved to death."

"Is that it?"

"For the moment," replied Mrs. Sheppard. "I can only imagine the circumstances she lived under. Mrs. Pepper has new and old scars all over her body. Someone has been beating her for a very long time."

"Yes, I saw some of the marks," replied Katherine. "Her husband is a no-good drunk, and he left her in a filthy shack with no food, water, or heat."

"It is a miracle the mother and baby survived," commented Mrs. Sheppard. "Men, they use us women. I see it every day."

"My husband is a kind, hard-working man," replied Katherine. "He and I will do our best to help."

"Doing this for that poor woman and her child is decent of you. And this will help the Indian, Raine, as well."

"I knew that Susan Pepper was in trouble. I feel bad I didn't help her earlier."

"You might have run into that man of hers and then…"

"That skunk! If he would have laid a hand on me…"

"The point is," said Mrs. Sheppard, "you came to Susan's rescue, and that's more than what most folks would do. I'll go now. I'll come back in a week to check up on her."

"What do I owe you?"

"I would like to make this a free one, but I'm in need of coin myself. So many of my patients promise to pay but don't. And often it's with eggs, or a chicken or…"

"How much?"

"Three dollars, please, and I thank you kindly."

Katherine Sharp did her best to care for the sick woman, but Susan Pepper developed a fever and then a cough. Her emaciated body tried to sweat the infection away, and it was going badly. The patient desperately needed nutritious food to recover but was too sick to eat. Sitting in the sick room, Katherine fed the baby goat's milk, and it seemed to be working. The wet nurse was to arrive in the morning.

Katherine was worried for the poor woman and didn't leave her. She placed cool, wet cloths on her fevered forehead and chest. That seemed to help, but then somewhere past midnight, Susan Pepper stopped breathing. She had suffered from too many beatings and too little food for far too long. Tom Sharp heard his wife's call of alarm and came into the bedroom.

"I'm sorry, Katherine," said Tom, hugging his wife. "You have nothing to be ashamed of. You did your best."

"But what will we do with the baby?"

"We'll care for him for as long as we can," said Tom. "What did the mother name him?"

"Christopher."

"Then he shall remain Christopher Pepper."

"His poor mother," said Katherine.

"Yes," said Tom, "the poor thing. If the father ever comes round, he'll have me to answer to."

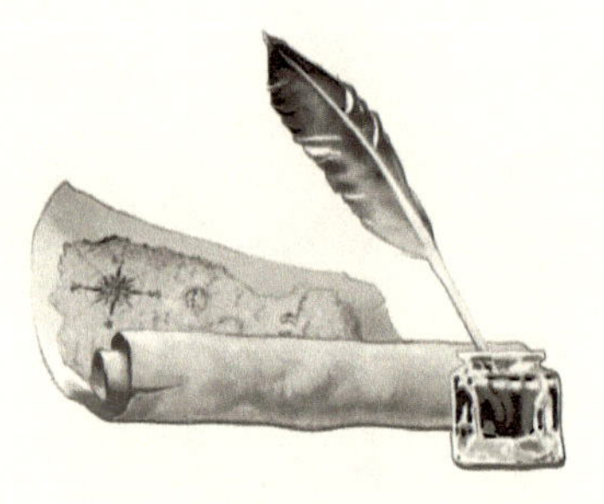

CHAPTER 14

Tom Sharp was in his trading post behind the counter folding blankets and putting them on a shelf. A very attractive dark-haired woman walked through the front door. She wore a long leather skirt, a floral printed blouse, a colorful shawl around her shoulders, and thick moccasins on her feet. She held a large parfleche bag in one hand and strapped to her back was a baby cradle. In it was a dark-haired, dark-eyed baby carefully wrapped in a blue blanket.

"Sir," said the woman, "I am the one called Raine. Are you Tom Sharp? I was sent by the midwife, Mrs. Sheppard. I am the wet nurse for baby Christopher."

"Yes, I'm Sharp. Your English is perfect, Raine."

"I was raised in Pueblo. I went to school and worked for the priest, Father Raverdy, as his housemaid."

"I see."

"I can cook, clean, clerk, read, write, and keep books. If you hire me to work for you and pay a fair wage, I can do all those things and help care for the baby as well."

"Ma'am, I don't know you. I would have to…"

"No problem, Mr. Sharp. You will see that I work hard and am congenial in doing so. Unless, of course, you have prejudice against an Indian?"

"Raine," said Sharp firmly, "you will find that my wife and I have no such prejudice. Most of my profit comes from trading for hides with the Utes. You do speak Ute?"

"I still speak my first tongue. I need steady work, a place to live for me and my baby."

"And your husband?" asked Sharp.

"He was hired by Goodnight to work his cattle. He was killed."

"I see," said Sharp. "My condolences, Raine."

"They say it was a ranching accident. And that is why I am here. Mrs. Sheppard said there may be…"

"Mrs. Sheppard assumed a lot, Raine. I thought you were here only for the baby. But it just so happens I do need the services of a clerk who can speak Ute. It would make things easier. And we have a room in the back for you and your child. This may be opportune for both of us."

"Does this mean you will hire me?"

"Yes."

"I am relieved. Now if you would take me to Christopher?"

"Of course. My wife and the child are in the back. She's been feeding him goat's milk. I will introduce you."

Katherine Sharp was sitting at the kitchen table, holding baby Christopher. Tom introduced Raine, and immediately the new employee put her parfleche on the floor, removed the cradle from her shoulders, and gently placed her child next to her bag.

"So you know, dear," said Tom, "I've hired Raine to work in the store. She speaks English perfectly and Ute. If you could set her and the child up with a room?"

"Tom, that's wonderful!"

"Mrs. Sharp," said Raine, "If Mr. Sharp will excuse us, I will nurse Christopher."

Saying that she began to unbutton her top, and Sharp quickly left the room.

"You must call me Katherine. Oh, what a beautiful baby!" said the trader's wife, pointing to the bright-eyed and silent child wrapped in the cradle. "What do you call…"

"It's a girl," replied Raine, "born a week before Christopher. She has the name her father wished, Crystal Stone."

"Has something happened…"

"Roger, my man, died working for Charles Goodnight."

"I am so sorry."

"I too."

Christopher took to the breast with vigor and began to suck.

"The boy is frail and hungry," said Raine. "We will soon take care of that."

"I'm pleased you are here."

"Perhaps, Mrs. Sharp, this will go well for both babies."

***

As promised, Mrs. Sheppard arrived for another visit but several days late.

"I have heard, Mrs. Sharp, that the mother, Susan Pepper died. I am sorry that I could not have come sooner."

Chapter 14

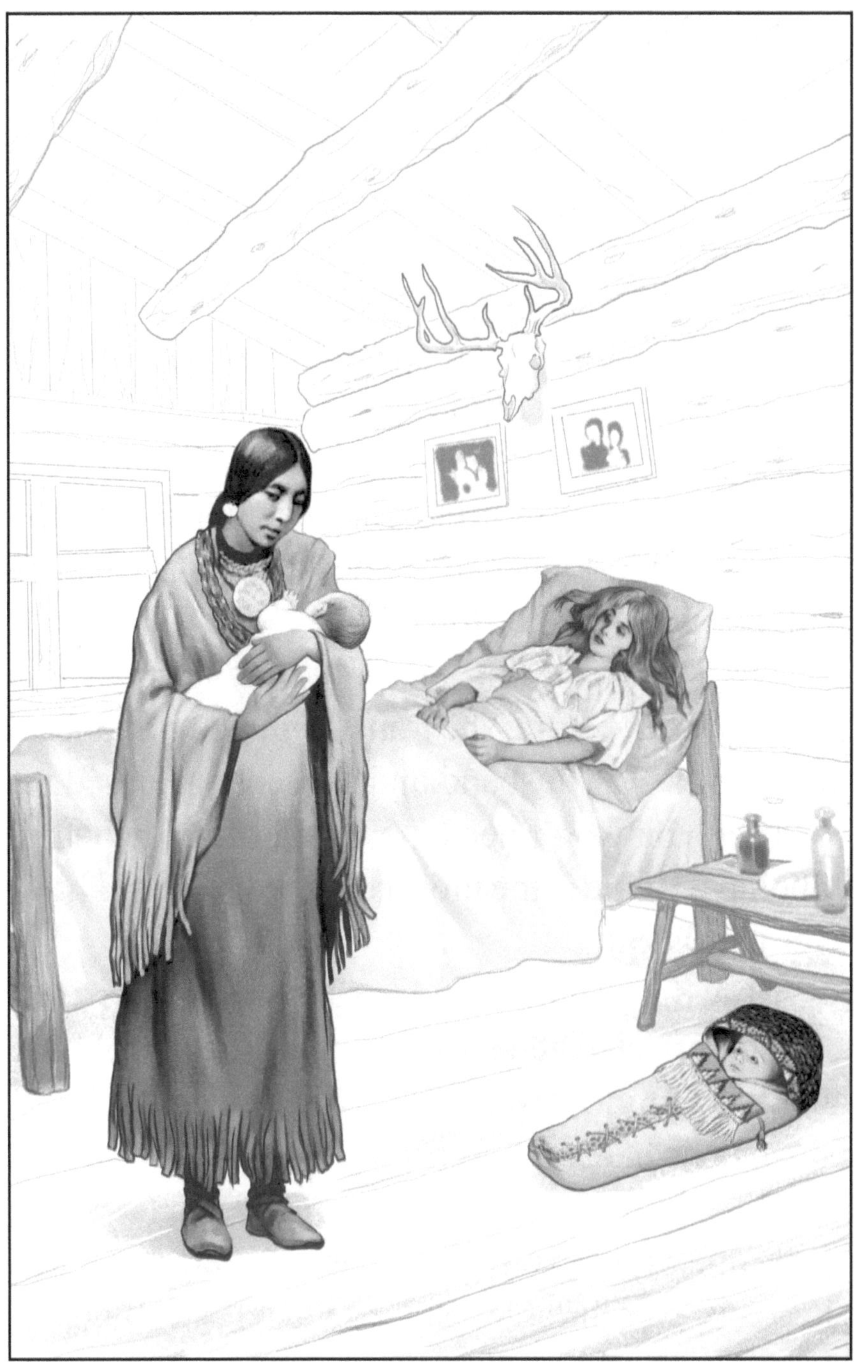

"She was so weak it was a miracle she was still alive when we found her," said Katherine.

"Well, I can examine the child, and then we can talk."

Going to the bedroom, Katherine and Mrs. Sheppard discovered Raine feeding Crystal. Finished, the Indian woman put her baby in a cradle and carried her out of the room.

"I see the child is much improved," said Mrs. Sheppard, "and no further complications. Raine is living and working here? She keeps both babies with her when in the store?"

"Yes," replied Mrs. Sharp. "Raine is smart and efficient. In the store, she translates and reorganizes the shelves. My husband and I are very pleased."

"I see you won't need me," said Mrs. Sheppard. "I believe Raine is the most educated woman I have ever met."

"How did you ever find her?" asked Katherine.

"The priest, Father Raverdy, in Pueblo told me about her in glowing terms. You may not know it, but she has had a rough life.

"Would you tell me?"

"Raine is a very private person. Perhaps when she feels comfortable, she might tell you herself.

What I know about her, I learned from the priest. Not to break confidence, I'll explain that when she was young, Apaches captured her. Chief Ouray rescued her as a teenager, but her tribe wouldn't allow her to return. Having no choice, the chief placed Raine with Father Raverdy, where she got her education. I'm afraid the whites in Pueblo were none too friendly, but I'll leave that to Raine to explain."

"And the poor woman lost her husband," said Katherine.

"Yes. If I may be so bold, Mrs. Sharp, I think Raine needs you as much as you need her. I could tell she is pleased to be here."

"I am happy to have her, and so is my husband. Thank you, Mrs. Sheppard."

"It is my great pleasure. She deserves a safe place to live. I'll be going now. Oh, and perhaps someday you'll need my services as well?"

Katherine laughed.

"Mrs. Sheppard, if the time comes, I will send for you."

"And I will be sure to be here."

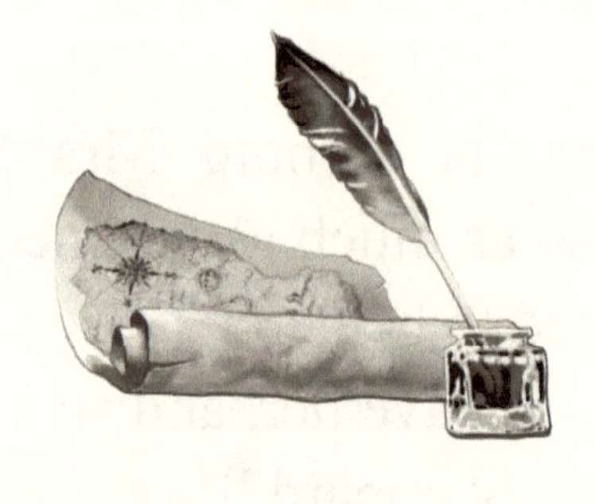

CHAPTER 15

Raine continued to be a complete revelation to the Sharps. She worked well with George Elmire. They spent all day and many nights together working in the store, counting inventory, loading, and unloading, and packing shelves.

Now, with Raine helping with commerce and translating, more Utes were coming with tanned hides. Business was good. With her encouragement, Sharp ordered more uniforms from Union and English surplus warehouses for trade.

Raine was everywhere. She was up early in the morning, cooked breakfast, fed Christopher and Crystal, then worked in the store. Those traveling through the Sangre de Cristo Pass to San Luis Valley and Taos stopped their wagon trains to purchase goods. With Raine and George Elmire handling much of the business, Sharp began to have more time to invest in horses and cattle.

***

"Raine, you've been here three months," said Sharp as the Indian woman set a large platter of fried eggs and ham on the table. "Each morning, you are up early, care for the babies, then cook. You never sit down or eat breakfast with us."

"Yes, we have asked you to join us many times," added Katherine.

"Have we done something that offends you?" continued Sharp.

"Oh, no, Mr. Sharp. I have a long list of items to complete in the store before we open and…"

"About that, too. How many times have I asked you to call me Tom?"

"You are my employer. I have been taught to mind my manners and my station in life."

"And what exactly is that?" asked Katherine.

"I am a wet nurse, a clerk, and an educated Ute woman. I admit that's a rarity. I learned from Father Raverdy that familiarity is forbidden to someone like me."

"Wrong!" said Katherine. "Since you have arrived, our lives have gone smoothly."

"That's right," added Tom. "You and George Elmire, together, have made our business grow and given us more time to enjoy life."

"I appreciate your trust," replied Raine. "But soon Mrs. Sharp will have a child. The birth will change both of you and your focus."

"All right," said Tom, "we give up. Just know we are happy you are here."

"And that goes for George Elmire," laughed Katherine. "Why, he follows you around like a lost puppy."

"I did not encourage him," said Raine. "My man, Roger Stone, is dead. I have no interest in another."

"Maybe you should tell George that," exclaimed Sharp.

"It is beginning to be a nuisance," said Raine. "I don't really know what…"

"If you don't like his attention," added Katherine, "tell him."

"I'm afraid it is time," replied Raine. "I will speak to George."

"You have a right to defend yourself from unwanted attention," said Sharp.

"Thank you," responded Raine. "Oh, I was going to tell you. Chief Ouray asked if you would object to his band camping along the Huerfano River."

“On my land?”

“Yes. Did you know your land has been our winter camp for generations?”

There was a long silence. Finally, Sharp answered.

“No. But I did know that all this land once belonged to the Utes. We make treaties, and then we break them.”

“Your people want it all,” said Raine.

“It seems that way. You tell Chief Ouray to bring his people, and it would be my honor for him to make winter camp on my land.”

“Good, Mr. Sharp,” said Raine. “He will be pleased.”

Tom Sharp sighed.

“Must you be so formal, Raine?”

“Yes, I must. Because of my past, I find it very hard to trust. Give me time. But I will tell you this, I am more in the white world than the Ute, and I will never take my children to a reservation. Chief Ouray also fears removal. Someday he will ask for our help to save his people. Help, I am afraid you and I will not have the power to give.”

***

Raine went back into the store, and after arranging a stack of clothing, she went to George Elmire.

"George," she said. "It is time we talked. There are no customers. Let us go out front and walk."

For the short period they worked together, both had remained reticent, George showing his affection by constantly trying to help Raine in her duties, often when she did not need the help. The rest of the time, he observed her with long adoring glances when he thought she was not looking. She was uncomfortably aware of it all.

They walked outside the Trading Post. Leading the way, Raine headed some distance from the store, where their conversation could not be overheard. As usual, some Ute Indians were sitting on the porch steps, others stood with their horses at the hitching rail, and still others were preparing to take hides inside for trade. Raine spoke to them in Ute and asked them to wait.

"George," said Raine. "Mister and Mrs. Sharp asked me to speak with you."

"They did?" said George. "I can't imagine what it is about. I am diligent in my work and in keeping the books."

"Yes, George, you are a loyal employee. They speak of you very highly. They…"

"Did you know that Tom Sharp saved my life?"

"No, I did not…"

"Yes, he and Pedro Gonzales found me beside the road with a broken leg. My horse and my possessions gone. I was at my end. I thought of nothing else but death. Tom talked me out of it and gave me this job."

"I didn't know that. I can see why you are so, as you say, diligent."

Raine walked in a straight line, George following. She stopped, turned, and walked back in the other direction. She kept repeating. Some thirty steps forward and back. George followed, saying nothing.

"Ahh, belated revelation! I know what it is now," said George. "I am a lonely old fool, and you are a very intelligent and desirable woman. I have the academic credentials, but in some ways, I think your knowledge of the world exceeds mine. A man like me is attracted more than anything else to intelligence. As far as you are concerned, I have overstepped my bounds. Have I not? Now that is the issue and why you have brought me out into the light of day. Is that not so?"

"George," said Raine, stopping her pacing abruptly, turning and facing the diminutive man. "I have this job, Christopher and Crystal to care for, and when I can, I help Chief Ouray and my people. That is all I can handle."

"You find me unacceptable material for a union," said the educated man.

"You assume too much, George. I was never available. My husband, Roger Stone, is the one man I loved. He is dead, but he is not gone in my memory. Do you understand?"

"It is because I am of little substance or stature?"

"George! You are not listening! Everything about you is admirable! I, too, admire intellect above all things. But…"

"You don't like my attention. My presence here is disturbing to your space and comfort."

"No, George. I was NEVER available. To you or any man. Stop your infatuation and accept me as a friend."

"I will leave tomorrow."

"George! That was never my intent!"

"All the same, it is time for me to move on."

"How will you do that?" asked Raine. "You work here for room and board. I could never understand that. One of your great education and to…"

"I owe Tom Sharp a great deal, but I am not a fool. Why bother him with little matters of an hourly wage?"

"George?"

"There is little cash trade, except when immigrants or travelers on the way to San Luis or Taos come through. The trading post never lost a thin dime, but I would charge extra for each item and take the coin for my salary. I believe it equals more than an hourly wage. And, I bet a modest amount on the many horse races that take place here, and I have won. Tomorrow I will leave and look for my own prospects."

"George, I did not mean to…"

"Not to worry, fair Raine. I shall seek fortune and affection in more auspicious circumstances."

"I should never have spoken to you."

"No, Raine, in matters of the heart, fate always plays a role."

"I am truly sorry."

"To quote my dear Tennyson," said George Elmire. "Tis better to have loved and lost than never to have loved at all."

"George, you are always so intense."

"Say nothing to our benefactor. I would like to slip away with my newly acquired horse, my dignity, and my accumulated wealth intact."

"You make it worse for me," replied Raine.

"Dear lady," laughed George. "Give me this bit of self-indulgence. I was content to admire from afar. It was not I that started this confrontation regarding unrequited love."

"George," said Raine and smiled. "I cannot tell if you are jesting or serious."

"Both, my love. Both."

"George!"

"Excuse me, my dear, once again, I exceed my boundaries. Allow me this one impertinence. Let me go and prepare for my departure. Make excuses for me. Tell Tom Sharp I am not feeling well. Tell him…it is a touch of the ague. But in truth, dear lady, it is head and heart that suffers."

True to his word, in the early morning, George Elmire secretly departed and disappeared.

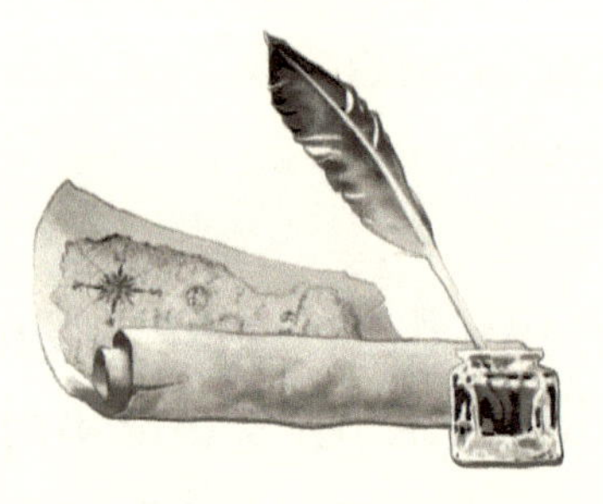

CHAPTER 16

Chief Ouray brought his band to the post, and there were hundreds. Tom Sharp met them and wondered what he had gotten himself into. Riding with the Ute chief, Tom led him to a suitable campsite along the river. Within minutes of arriving, travois and horses were beginning to be unloaded, and tipis were set up in a traditional pattern not too far from the water.

"Some of my people still build wickiups," said Ouray.

"I have seen them," said Tom. "Poles are cut, leaned against a living tree, and covered."

"The tipi we learned to use on the plains," said the chief.

"You speak English very well, Chief."

"It is necessary. I have to deal with devious white men."

The trader laughed.

"There are certainly many of those," said Sharp.

"We must talk further after my people are settled," suggested Ouray. "Raine said you were a good man. It is well that we saved you that day when the Apaches wanted your scalp. And you helped me when you declared our horse the winner in that big race. I came here for peace and to save the band I have left. So often a tribe member disappears, is hurt, or killed. It is hard now to live on our own land since the whites have come."

"Then I am glad you are here," said Sharp.

"For a long time, you have been trading with my people. You provide them with food, tools, tobacco, and clothing in trade for the hides. And…"

"Yes?"

"You have blue uniforms. My men like the color, the look, and the feeling it gives them."

"You object?"

"No. I thought if I trade you a buffalo robe, you would pick out one for a chief, a coat with yellow fringe on the shoulders and many brass buttons."

Sharp laughed.

"You mean with epaulets?"

"Ep-pa-lets?"

"Yes, that is what those shoulder ornaments are called."

"You trade? Make the chief look good?"

"Yes," laughed Tom. "I will give you an entire uniform, striped pants and a fancy British Officer's jacket. It would be my pleasure. No buffalo robe necessary."

"Good. Then after, we sit down, smoke pipe, and talk about friendship. You will help me keep my people safe."

"Chief," said Tom, "as long as I have the power and ability, you can camp here."

***

Sharp watched the camp and tried to understand how the Utes prepared for winter. When he had questions, he called in Raine, and she explained.

"The warriors separate," she said. "They ride out on the plains and up in the mountain passes. They shoot antelope, mule deer, and buffalo. The men catch fish and salt or smoke a good supply. The women make and store jerky, and they grind corn and wheat. Whites and Spanish families learn from us and copy Indian methods. But many of the whites have one advantage over the Indians: they raise cattle."

"Then why don't the Indians learn from us?" asked Sharp.

"Who would let an Indian have a herd and brand cattle?" asked Raine. "Mister Sharp, you say you understand, but you don't. The whites keep coming, and they want us dead and gone."

"You seem to be very close to Ouray."

"I am. He is my chief."

"I'm curious. What do you talk about when you visit?"

"You want to know if we conspire against you?" Raine replied tersely. "We do not. I teach the chief what Father Raverdy taught me."

"And the chief wants to learn these things?"

"Yes. He says he wants to know all he can about the white world."

"He thinks he can find a way to save your people?" asked Sharp.

"He has always tried to educate himself. There is a reason they call him the peace chief. Against the wishes of other Ute leaders, he signed peace treaties. He did it to keep the people from being killed or sent to reservations."

"I understood some of that," said Sharp.

"Chief Ouray has always made calculated decisions. Did you know other Ute tribes hate him for signing and won't listen to him?"

"Unfortunate. I didn't know that."

"It is," responded Raine. "In many ways, Chipeta, his wife, is his equal. She has sat on other Ute councils to keep the peace with other Ute bands, where Chief Ouray is no longer accepted. Both have worked to keep the people safe."

"That I didn't know," said Sharp.

"Hence, the chief is always educating himself. He realizes the whites are too powerful for our people to fight. He has seen your cities and knows that resistance means death."

"I don't agree with what is happening," said Sharp.

"It is fortunate for our tribe," said Raine, "that the Arapahos and Cheyenne were rounded up and put on reservations."

"But that doesn't take care of the Apaches," said Sharp. My neighbors come to me, afraid when your tribe fights bloody skirmishes with other Indians."

"Some things cannot be stopped," said Raine. "That is one of them."

"If your people continue to fight, then their removal to reservations will come even sooner."

"I know," replied the woman. "Not all of the Utes will go peacefully."

Raine returned to stocking shelves. Sharp thought that an awful lot had changed in just one week. He stepped outside onto the porch. At the same time, John White and John Williams rode up to the hitching rail. Dismounting and pushing for room among a group of Ute's with hides to trade, they tied reins.

"We've gotta talk!" demanded Williams.

'You sound upset," said Sharp coming off the porch.

"We are," said White.

The three ranchers walked some distance from the post.

"What the devil do you think you're doing?" asked Williams.

"You mean about the Indian encampment?"

"You're darn right," exclaimed Williams. "Why man, my neighbors, White and Spanish, are furious."

"Chief Ouray wanted a safe place for his people. Long before the government took their land, this was their winter camp."

"So you let them return?" asked White.

"I did. The chief said each year, members of his tribe disappear or are killed. He thinks his people will be safer by camping on my land."

"Didn't you know that would upset your neighbors?"

"I suspected," said Sharp, "but what could I do? Don't you remember? Those few years ago when the chief and his band saved us from the Apaches?"

"We do."

"Now he is asking for my help, and I gave it to him. You two should support me in this."

"You do know how to turn the worm, don't you?" said White in disgust.

"All right," said Williams. "We'll talk it up that they are here for a safe winter camp. But you better make sure they don't fight any battles with the Apaches, or it'll go bad for you and them."

After their conversation, Tom Sharp watched his friends go to their horses and ride away.

***

What Sharp could not stop was the war-like behavior of the Utes. They were always on guard for their enemies. For protection against the Apaches,

Ute warriors took turns up on Sheep Mountain. When their enemies were spotted, the Utes sent smoke signals by day and fire signals by night. It was a constant war between these factions, and the Utes never backed down. The settlers all across the county hated it when Ute warriors whooped and hollered through the night, preparing for a raid. Worse, they saw the warriors in war paint, taking scalps and coming back bloodied. No matter what Tom Sharp said to Chief Ouray, he could not stop him. What most concerned Sharp was how could the Utes find peace with the whites if they continued conflict with the Apaches?

CHAPTER 17

On a Saturday evening in May, 1872, Katherine fixed a candlelight and wine dinner for her husband.

"What's the special occasion?" asked Tom. "I don't mind getting dressed up and sitting down to a fancy dinner, but you have to admit, even for you, this is very unusual."

"Tom, let's just be romantic tonight. Promise me you won't talk about the trading post, horses, cattle, or business. Tonight let's just concentrate on each other."

"Yes, my dear," he replied with a grin. "I shall be at my most gracious. Such an inviting request cannot be ignored. And what man in his right mind would not pay attention to the fairest and most attractive beauty in southern Colorado?"

"No need to overdo it, Tom."

"But I do mean it. I have such a lovely and intelligent wife."

"And I," said Katherine, "when I do see him, have such a charming and clever husband. Just wait, and I'll serve dinner."

Katherine brought a roast with potatoes, mushrooms, and carrots to the table and poured wine. For dessert, there was apple pie.

"Please remain seated, Tom, while I clear the dishes."

She returned with another bottle of wine.

"My dear," said Tom, "I do believe you have something important to tell me."

Katherine filled the two glasses and sat down beside him. She took his hand and smiled.

"Now that you are doing so well at business, and we seem to have so few worries, what is it that you would like next?"

"Katherine!" exclaimed Tom. "You're going to have a baby!"

"Yes…"

Tom jumped up from his chair, went to his knees next to his wife, and kissed her. He continued kissing her lovingly and with great warmth. Finally, he paused and looked into her eyes.

"Katherine, I couldn't have any greater news in the world! I am so happy! Are you happy, too, my dear?"

"Yes, of course. Can't you tell? This is the reason I thought to make this evening special."

"You have done that, my wonderful woman. Oh, you must be more careful from now on. I can hire someone to help you with the housework so you can rest and…"

"Raine is quite enough help, Tom. But before we celebrate the rest of the evening, I need you to agree on something."

"Yes, anything!"

"No, you don't understand. I am concerned by the lack of medical care here. It's not that I don't trust the midwife, Mrs. Sheppard, but I would like to be under a doctor's care. A good one. And, I haven't seen my parents in a long time, and I…"

"You want to go back to Missouri and have the baby there?"

"Yes…"

"But Katherine, I can't come with you. I have so much to do here and…"

"When the baby comes due, sometime in November, I think, you can come then. After, when the baby is ready, we can travel back here together."

"I can't say I like it, and it will be very lonely. I will be so worried, but if you think it is the best choice, go. But my dearest, to appease me, can you think of something pleasant for tonight?"

"Oh, I believe I can manage that," said Katherine, smiling broadly.

***

On November 25th, 1872, in Marion County, Missouri, Mrs. Katherine Sharp delivered a healthy baby boy, William. The grandparents, Mr. & Mrs. Durrett, and Tom Sharp, were there for the birth. A few weeks later, Tom, Katherine, and the baby traveled by train and then stagecoach to Walsenburg. From there, Pedro, Tom's freight driver, took them by buggy back to Buzzard Roost Trading Post. Caring for the baby, and dealing with business, the community, and Utes, was a blur of activity and made four years pass quickly for the Sharps. Two more children, Elizabeth and Emma, were born in those years.

Under the guidance of Captain Deus and Tom Sharp, the largest employers in the community, the settlers prospered, the population grew, and conditions improved. Down the road, a schoolhouse

Chapter 17

was built in Gardner, and a teacher, Aaron Wilburn, was hired. Raine, Crystal, and Christopher lived behind the trading post in George Elmire's cabin. Both children were now five years old, and the year was 1876.

***

Katherine grew increasingly upset with her husband's absence. She and the children barely saw him through the day or at night. Everyone demanded his time. Williams and White were married now and raising families of their own. They were always asking for help with their ranches. Tom's horse and cattle business took him to Denver and other states, and sometimes he was gone weeks at a time. Because of his constant absence, she decided to do something to keep her husband at home.

"Tom," said Katherine one evening after dinner. "What do you think about Friday evening get-togethers with your friends?"

"What did you have in mind?" he asked.

"You're gone a lot. You see your friends and do your work, and I'm here all alone with the children. Perhaps we could invite those closest to you to Friday night dinners. That way, we could spend more time together."

"I'm sorry, Katherine, but my absences are necessary. I…"

"I know, dear, but I just thought if we had gatherings, we could all become much closer."

"It's a fine idea. But don't you think every Friday would be a bit much?"

"Then every other Friday?" said Katherine.

"Fine. But how will you invite them?"

"Give me a few minutes to write an invitation, and then tell me what you think?"

She found paper and pencil, went to the kitchen table, and began writing. When finished, she gave it to her husband.

Dear Captain and Mrs. Deus &Family,

This coming Friday, you are invited to dinner at our home. After supper, the children will be entertained with toys & games, and the adults with amicable conversation, drinks, and card games. We hope you and other invited friends and families will have a cordial time. If successful, in the spirit of camaraderie, this may become a regular event every other Friday throughout the year.

Sincerely,

Thomas and Katherine Sharp

"You have been planning this, haven't you? Well, my dear, what you have written here could not be any more perfect."

The very first dinner was a great success. Present were White, Williams, their wives and children, Captain Deus and his family, as well as Pedro Gonzales, the wagon driver, and his wife. Raine and her two children also attended. After a hearty meal, the youngsters were entertained with blocks and board games.

Around the dinner table, the men played cards. Captain Deus was very skilled at poker, and the men made small wagers.

"Coffee or tea, anyone?" offered Katherine.

Tom poured cold beer into mugs and opened a large whiskey bottle.

The women sat and talked. In this manner, a comfortable evening was spent.

Raine, to her astonishment, liked these gatherings. It was the closest thing to family. She was able to relax as much as she ever had in the company of others. She enjoyed seeing her girl and boy play peacefully on the floor with the other children.

After one of the gatherings, Raine returned to her cabin. She lay in bed with her children on either side of her. Unable to sleep, the young woman thought about George Elmire. She felt bad that she caused him to leave those few years ago. Since he left, her work had doubled. Keeping the books was an added aggravation. Raine lay quietly and wrestled with her one constant worry. *What will become of my children and me?*

The following day she got up, fed Crystal and Christopher, and taking them with her to work, she went about her duties. A playroom was close so she could constantly check on the youngsters. When it was time for school, Katherine brought Billy to her. Taking the boy and her children, Raine boarded a buggy and drove to the school house in Gardner. Then, she returned to the store. At noon, she shared lunch with Katherine and her daughters, Elizabeth and baby Emma.

For the two women, this was their daily routine throughout the year.

***

As the Friday evening dinners progressed, Raine relaxed further. Sometimes she played cards with

Captain Deus, Williams, White, and Sharp. She caught on quickly to the rules of the game and even won a few hands. They were playing penny poker, and Sharp gave her coins to bet with. She laughed when she won. Unusual for her, she took sips from a glass containing whiskey and water. She liked the strong taste. A strange warm feeling came over her, and she became more loquacious. That night her banter and joking matched and perhaps even exceeded the wit of the four men.

When the dinner party broke up, Raine remained. Her two children and the Sharp youngsters had fallen asleep on the carpet amongst their toys and games.

"Raine, I have never seen you like this," said Katherine. "You seem happy."

"Perhaps it is the drink," laughed Raine. "No, it is more than that. I find it so relaxing to be here. I enjoy these evenings very much."

"That's good," said Tom. "We're glad you feel comfortable."

"That's it," replied Rain. "Comfortable and safe. I worry so about Crystal and Christopher and their futures. I want them to be secure and have a good life. I worry that my heritage may jeopardize their happiness. I…"

"We told you long ago," said Katherine, "that you are family. We will watch out for you and them. We didn't expect it, but you became Christopher's mother. I made promises to myself, and then it just worked out that you took over when Bill was born. And I am so grateful for that. I really am."

"You never shared much with us, Raine," said Sharp. "We've always wondered."

"I would not want to burden you," replied Raine in her old formal way.

"Haven't you heard us talk about our lives?" asked Katherine. "You know all about us, but we know so little about you. Isn't that what friends do? Share burdens?"

"I've never said much about my life to anyone except Father Raverdy and Chief Ouray," began Raine. "But I did want to explain some things to you. After I was captured by the Apaches, it was very difficult. They adopted me and put me to work. I was young, and I quickly learned their language. It was hard. Often, we did not have enough food. We were always changing camp and running from enemies, both Indian and white. Then, when I was thirteen, Chief Ouray attacked and got me back in a raid. But the Ute people, they would not accept me."

"That's awful," said Katherine. "Why did they reject you?"

"I was dressed as an Apache woman, spoke Apache, and temporarily had forgotten some of my Ute language. They thought of me as their enemy and treated me badly."

"That must have been even harder on you," said Katherine."

"It was. But Chief Ouray, he came to me. He said he arranged with the priest, Father Raverdy, to take me in with the Sisters of Charity in Pueblo. They ran a school and found a place for me to stay. But in some ways, that was harder."

"Why was that?" asked Tom. "Isn't that where you learned to speak English and received your education?"

"Yes," replied Raine. "But they were very strict, and the other students, well…they were rough on an Indian girl."

"I see," said Katherine. "Is that when Father Raverdy helped you?"

"He took me in as his housemaid. I advanced very quickly in school. Then Father Raverdy gave me books the Sisters did not teach. I would read one, and then the good Father would discuss its content and meaning in the evenings. He called it my advanced studies."

"It sounds intriguing," said Katherine. "We favor education. Then what happened?"

"Each year, people in the church gossiped about an Indian housekeeper living in the same residence of Father Raverdy. When I turned eighteen, they demanded I leave. The priest did not want me to go, but I did, and I…I'm sorry," said Raine. "Suddenly, I feel very tired and dizzy. Perhaps, we can speak of this another night?"

"Yes, of course," said Katherine. "Tom, please help Raine take the children back to the cabin."

"Yes, certainly," said Sharp, "but honestly, Raine, it will be difficult to wait to hear the rest of your story."

"Tom!" exclaimed Katherine, giving him a dark look.

"I'm sorry," said Raine, "it is late. Perhaps next time."

Raine gently awakened Christopher and lifted Crystal off the floor. Sharp helped them back to the cabin. That night, before falling asleep, Raine thought about what she had told the Sharps. It was astonishing that she felt no remorse for revealing parts of her past life.

***

The daily routine continued for Raine and the Sharp family. But if anything, Katherine and Tom seemed to be even more cordial. After some discussion, a plan was made by Sharp to add to her cabin so the children could have their own bedrooms.

At the next Friday gathering, all of the guests returned. The children of Captain Deus, Frank and Pete, took the younger ones to entertain in the playroom. Raine stayed with the women and participated in polite conversation. She played chess with Juanita Deus and, not liking beer, sipped cautiously on whiskey. Once again, when the party broke up, Raine remained behind, Christopher and Crystal fast asleep in the other room.

"I have thought so much about what you told us about your past life," Katherine said. "I've wondered how you survived all that happened to you."

"And, as I said before," added Tom, "I find it intriguing that Chief Ouray sent you to school in Pueblo and that you taught the chief what you learned."

“That last time we talked,” said Raine, “I did leave out a lot. Do you really want to hear me…”

“Yes!” exclaimed both Katherine and Tom.

“Tom,” said Raine. “Father Raverdy would lend me a buggy, and when our band was at winter camps, I visited the chief. I would take my notes, maps, and books I was loaned by the priest. Chipeta was interested too, and often she would sit and listen. But it was the chief who led the questions. I would show Chief Ouray maps of North America and South America. I showed him the United States and Colorado. He was interested in the railroads, the states’ names, and where Washington DC was located on the map.”

“He really wanted to learn all that?” asked Sharp.

“Yes. He told me he wanted to know what I learned at the school and from the priest. I couldn’t teach him everything, but slowly over the years, I shared a lot. He was rather intrigued by maps of the world, the fact that it was round, and how that was even possible. He thought the other countries in the world must be amazing places. I tried to teach him an overview of current governments, their histories, and languages. The chief was a good student.”

"I'm astounded," said Tom. "There is more to the Ute leader than I ever imagined."

"Mister Sharp," said Raine, "most whites underestimate the Indian. Just because most live in tipis and live a nomadic life does not mean we are stupid. Chief Ouray was always thinking beyond the present."

"Like in a chess game?" asked Sharp.

"Exactly," replied Raine.

"The last time we spoke," said Katherine, "you said you were forced out of the priest's employment. That must have been hard. Where did you go next?"

"And how did you meet your husband?" added Sharp.

"Tom!" exclaimed Katherine.

"I took a job with a merchant in Walsenberg. He didn't pay me much but provided a small cabin behind his store for me to live in. At first, I served customers, but they hated an Indian waiting on them, so he had me stay out of sight. At night I did the books and helped stock shelves."

"At least you were kept safe," said Katherine.

"I know Father Raverdy was worried, and he often checked up on me. But there was a time when I was attacked and..."

“You never told me,” said Tom. “Was that…”

“Tom!” interrupted Katherine, “let her tell it in her own way.”

“I think I have talked myself out,” said Raine. “This is hard for me. Perhaps another night?”

“Raine!” said Tom. “This is so exasperating! Must you leave now!”

“Tom Sharp!” exclaimed Katherine. “For heaven’s sake, be quiet!”

“Yes, dear,” replied Tom as he smiled and winked at Raine.

***

Every workday, Raine would have lunch with Katherine. After their meal, Elizabeth and Emma would be put down for a nap. The older children were at school. One week after the last Friday night dinner, Tom joined the women for lunch. He was eager to hear what else Raine had to say about her past life. Remaining in the kitchen, the three adults continued their conversation over coffee.

“The last time,” began Tom, “you told us you were attacked. Could you…”

"Tom!" exclaimed his wife in defense of the Indian woman.

"It's all right, Katherine," said Raine. "I will tell you how it was."

"See!" said Tom, looking at his wife for vindication.

"It was such a vivid memory, and I recall it exactly as it happened," said Raine. "I know it might be strange, but if I close my eyes, I can remember every word and detail."

Tom and Katherine waited, saying nothing, and Raine began to speak.

"It was late afternoon when I first met my husband, Roger Stone. I was bringing a basket of food to my cabin when two men accosted me. They were drunken and smelly cowhands. My employer insisted I dress in a typical woman's work dress, and my hair was done up like any white woman. But my darker skin and black hair revealed my circumstance of birth."

"Yes?" said Katherine, unable to help herself.

Raine continued.

"Where are you going, Indian?" said one of the aggressors.

"Home," I said, "let me be!"

"The cowboy reeked of alcohol, dirty, smelly, and unshaven. He grabbed my left arm and pulled me close. I was taught to fight as a child. I dropped my basket and, cupping my right hand, drove my palm up under the man's chin. His head jerked up, and he fell hard in the dirt and did not get up."

His drunken friend was angry.

"Say, you!" he said. "You can't treat my pal like that."

"The cowboy raised a fist and struck at me, but I ducked and kicked the drunken fellow in the groin."

"Atta girl," exclaimed Tom.

"He, too, fell to the ground," continued Raine. "The first assailant recovered, grabbed for a knife at his waist, and stood up. That was when a third man appeared. He drew a pistol and clubbed the knife wielder from behind. Once again, the fellow hit the ground, but he did not get up this time."

"I'm sorry, Ma'am," said the stranger to me. "These hands are drunk and out of their heads. They shouldn't have bothered you."

"Thank you," I told him. "I'm not sure I could have defended myself against the knife."

"You did good," said the cowboy. "He asked me, 'where did you learn to fight like that?'"

"Can't you see I am an Indian?" I replied

"A right purty lady, Ma'am, and smartly dressed, too," he told me.

"We introduced ourselves. He said his name was Roger Stone. I told him my name was Raine."

"An unusual but pretty name," he said.

"I told him, 'I suppose so.'"

"Roger knelt down and picked up fallen packages and put them in my basket, and rising, handed it to me. I'll never forget how Roger saved my life, and it is the reason I can recall what happened word for word."

"Astonishing," said Katherine. "I can see why you would remember."

"Well," said Tom, "could you tell us what else happened?"

"The two men worked for Roger, and they asked for money. He refused. He told them they let the cattle run down a fence, and in the first two weeks, all they did was eat food and take up space. He fired them. Then they called him an Indian lover and threatened his life. Roger hit one, and when the other pulled a knife, he dared him to use it. The fellow backed down, and then both men wandered off, very angry."

"Roger Stone sounds like a right capable man," said Sharp.

"Oh, he was," said Raine. "I do miss him so."

"Certainly, there must be more," said Katherine.

"Yes. Roger invited me to dinner at the hotel, and I told him I wasn't welcome. He got upset and said he would make sure they would serve me. I said, 'Why cause trouble?' He kept asking me to dinner. Finally, I told him there was this little Mexican place down the road that served good food, and there I would be welcome. After that, Roger met me often. To tell the truth, he wouldn't take no for an answer. He was very kind. He said his mother was a strong, educated woman and that he liked that about me too. To tell the truth, he just swept me off my feet. He asked me to marry him, but I told him first I had to speak to Father Raverdy."

"And then you got married?" asked Tom.

"It wasn't quite that simple, but yes. Father Raverdy pointed out to Roger that our life wouldn't be easy. Nor would it be for our children. He told the priest that didn't matter and that he loved me and would not stop until we were married."

"And?" said Katherine.

"Father Raverdy went on about how special I was. That someday women would be equal to men and that I should be a teacher or somebody in the government. Roger said he didn't care about that. He just wanted to marry me and take care of me."

"Wish I could have met him," said Tom.

"I wish that, too," replied Raine. "We were married in a private ceremony by Father Raverdy and with only one witness. The priest didn't want to cause conflict in the community. And then Roger took me to Goodnight's Rock Canyon Ranch, near Pueblo. We had a wonderful time together. Often he would take me with him to move cattle to water and better grass. No other man was like him. Every moment together was exciting. He accepted me for who I was, and I don't ever think he thought of me as an Indian. I became pregnant, and he insisted I stay home. Then one day, his men came to me, hat in hand, and said Roger died in a horse accident."

"And that is how you eventually came to us?" asked Katherine, wiping her eyes.

"Yes," replied Raine.

"Thank you for telling us your story," said Katherine. "All these years, we wondered."

"Yes," added Tom. "We're so fortunate to have you as a worker and a friend."

When Raine took the children to their cabin that night, they fell quickly to sleep. She lay in bed and thought once again about her past.

Later, Raine's reverie was disturbed by Crystal.

"Mommy, water."

Christopher also woke, put his small hands on Raine's shoulder, and pushed.

"Me too, Mummy. Water."

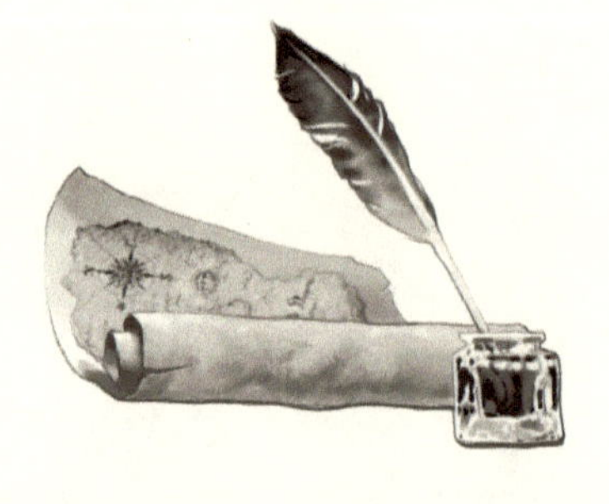

CHAPTER 18

It was Sunday, the day that Raine always visited Chief Ouray. She and her children were having dinner with the Sharps.

"Raine," said Tom, "would you mind taking me with you to visit Chief Ouray today?"

"Of course," responded the young woman. "The chief would like that."

Raine left her children in the care of Katherine. Taking a buggy, Sharp drove the two of them down to the Indian camp along the river. They met Ouray and his wife, Chipeta, at the chief's tipi. For an hour they talked about harvesting food and how successful they might be.

"My men are having trouble locating buffalo," said the chief. "It may be a long winter."

"Chief," said Sharp. "Trade has been good this year, and my cattle are doing well. I would be honored to offer you six steers for your people."

"Sharpy is a good man," said Ouray. "That meat will go a long way."

When the hour was over, they said their goodbyes, and Tom and the girl climbed aboard the buggy and left for the trading post.

***

That night Chief Ouray lay down in the bedding next to his wife. Eventually, Chipeta asked him directly what had been on her mind for a very long while.

"My man, you use that girl, Raine. Why?"

"She is strong. Do you not see it? After all these years, you question this now?"

"I thought I understood, but now I am not sure."

"My woman, trust me. What she brings to us will be of great import to our tribe."

"How?"

"Raine has already survived three worlds. Ours of the Ute, of the Apache, and now the world of the whites. The priest taught her much. In turn, that girl teaches me. We must learn as much as we can."

Chapter 18

"I understand all of that. What confuses me is what she teaches you about other countries and people. How does that help us?"

"Woman, I must learn all I can about where these whites come from. Why they are stronger and of greater numbers. If we are to keep what we have left, we must know all we can."

"And this young woman will do that for you?"

"Where else can I learn it?"

"When more whites turn against us, will Sharpy help us?"

"I believe so. He lets us camp along the river."

"But it is our land."

"No longer, wife. The white government gave it away."

"It is wrong."

"Yes, it is so. But in speaking of Sharpy, he trades with our people when no one else will. He is honest. You remember the horse race?"

"It was close."

"He stood up for us when we won. That money has gone far. We still have some left to buy supplies."

"It is not easy," said Chipeta.

"No, wife, it is not. Only because of you are we still speaking with the northern tribes. They hate me for signing the peace treaties. You are the first woman to sit in council and speak with the other chiefs. They listen to you and no longer hear my words."

"I defended you because I believed you did the right thing," said Chipeta. "You signed those treaties to save Ute lives."

"Yes, but they only know that through you. I need you, wife, even more than you need me."

"It is kind of you to say. You have always been a good, strong man."

"Sometimes it is the stronger thing to have peace than to fight and die in battles we cannot win. It is because we cannot fight that I am afraid."

"Of what?"

"Each year, more whites come. Each year we lose game and hunting grounds. Braves are killed, and we are pushed back. Someday, they will push harder, and like other tribes, we will be removed far from our lands."

"My love, I wish to never live to see that day."

"And I, dear wife."

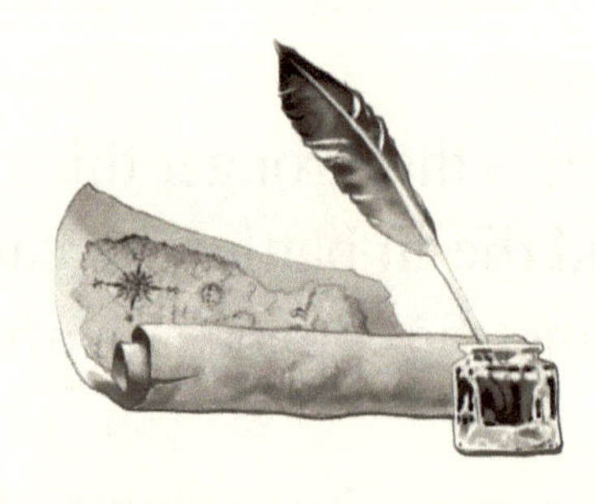

CHAPTER 19

Raine continued to work for Tom and Katherine Sharp at the Trading Post. Katherine was helping as much as she could with the business, but her three children kept her busy. Together, the two women shared child care and, away from the trading post, volunteered in the community to help others. They did much charity work for the school in Gardner and held fundraising activities.

Sharp helped his friends, Williams and White. Together they were doing well in selling their stock. The stamping mill was still running, and Buzzard Roost Trading Post continued to benefit from the Ute hide trade. Sharp became even wealthier. A shipment of white-faced Herefords was improving his cattle herd. And the thoroughbred/mustang foals developed strong trail horses that could jump anything. The businessman's reputation as a horse breeder increased.

"We need more horses," said Sharp while visiting his friends White and Williams.

"What do you have in mind?" asked White.

"We need better horses. Remember what we talked about way back in Cheyenne?"

"What's that?" asked Williams.

"Having a working ranch, earning money off our cattle and horses, expanding as far as we can."

"You're already doing that," said White. "Heck, you're way past us. You run that stamping mill, the trading post, you're breeding and selling horses from Taos to Denver, and have improved cattle herds. How can we beat that?"

"That's why I'm here," said Sharp. "Let's get some new stock for our ranches. The nags around the county and state put their riders to shame. Why, up in Idaho there are some of the grandest and biggest Indian ponies you ever saw."

"Like White said," exclaimed Williams. "You're already doing that."

"I'm giving you a chance to breed better stock. We'll have some of the finest hunting and riding horses in the territory with this new bunch."

"How many head are you talking about?" asked Williams.

"Two hundred and twenty-five tough wild ponies!"

"Two hundred and twenty-five?" said White. "Are you nuts?"

"Have I failed either one of you yet?" laughed Sharp.

"How much?" asked Williams. "We couldn't afford that lot."

"Well, I want to give both of you a chance to purchase as many as you can," said Sharp.

"And what about grass?" asked White. "Before, we had plenty of grass, but those Spanish are moving thousands of sheep across the dead line and eating our graze. I've confronted them, and so far, they just keep coming. And, unlike you, Tom, we can't afford to buy cut grass for our herds."

"Yeah, that is a problem," said Sharp. "We definitely have to find a clever way to stop that. We don't want to go to war with the Spanish. If they turn against us, we'd lose everything we have."

"That's not the only problem," said Williams. "We've got mountain lions that's killing stock. I've had a man shooting them over bait piles, and if anything, I'm losing more cattle and foals than before."

"You two should have come to me sooner about this. After we settle the order on those Indian ponies, we need to work together on the catamount and sheep problem. So how about it? How many are you two in for?"

The horses were shipped by rail. Tom Sharp ended up with the majority. Once branded and out on open range, grass was beginning to be a problem. The sheepherders were moving in, and their giant flocks decimated the land. Overgrazing was occurring, and with such little rainfall, the grassland was turning to dirt. Something would have to be done.

The mountain lions continued to be a problem. Sharp, a renowned rifle shot, his sharpshooting known to the Indians and local residents, took stand over bait. In one month, he had killed fourteen cougars, and a couple of them were of enormous size. Still, it didn't seem to totally stop the predation. But, overgrazing of grass and the growing sheep herd was their worst problem.

The three men coming together at Sharp's ranch mounted up. They were intent on confronting the worst sheep herder crossing over the dead line. Open graze that had been used by Williams, White, and Sharp since setting up their homesteads was now being eaten by thousands of sheep.

"Let me do the talking," said Sharp.

"Wouldn't expect anything less," said John White, getting astride his horse and then spitting.

"Yeah, you seem to always take the lead," replied Williams.

"Look, I know our anger's up," said Sharp. "If you think either of you can handle this better than me, go at it."

"No, you've made your point," replied Williams.

"Get this," said Sharp. "If we knock around or kill any of these sheep herders, every Spanish-speaking person in the entire country will turn against us. Let us have our say. If it doesn't go well, we'll find another way."

"And what would that be?" asked White. "We're losing grass, and we've got to act soon."

"Like I said," replied Sharp. "We'll think of something."

It was summer, and Antonio Archuleta was at the top of a mountain meadow guarding his sheep. It looked like a flock of thousands busily eating the grass. Surrounding the sheep, cattle belonging to the three ranchers grazed. The men had no choice but to ride through the middle of the flock. Sheep split and scattered as Sharp led his two friends to confront the sheep herder.

"You scatter my sheep!" complained Archuleta.

"Yes, we do," replied Sharp from atop his mount. "And you, sir, are letting your flock graze the grass down to dirt."

"It is free range, Señor Sharp. There are no fences. You cannot stop me or my sheep."

"We could if we wanted to!" shouted John Williams.

Williams spurred his horse at Archuleta. The man side-stepped and then whacked a leg of the mount with his long stick. This caused William's horse to snort and back up.

"Hold it!" ordered Sharp. "Williams is right. We could stop you, Antonio! You are the interloper here, and you know it. You are past the dead line, and you know that as well."

The sheepherder spit. Then he thumped the dirt with the staff.

"The dead line is meaningless. My people were here many years before you gringos come. Harm me or my sheep, and you will have trouble. In this country, we are more than you."

"Still," replied Sharp, "we come to warn you that your sheep are eating grass we have used for years for our horses and cattle. We move them and never overgraze. You cause trouble for both of us. There will be no grass for your sheep or our stock in the next years. The rain, especially in the low areas, comes infrequently, and you know that better than any of us."

"Go!" said Archuleta. "You have no say on open range."

"All right," replied Sharp. "We warned you. Remove your sheep!"

"What will you do if I don't?"

"We'll think of something," said Sharp. "You know that in this matter, you are in the wrong."

"You threaten me, señor?"

"Warning you. No man will harm you or your sheep. But we will find another way. And, we will let it be known what you are doing to the grass."

"Your words are meaningless to me. Leave, señor."

"All right," said Sharp, "we'll go. But know that this will not go well for you."

Sharp turned his magnificent mount, a cross between mustang and thoroughbred. Putting spurs to his horse, it leaped to a gallop through the middle of the gathered flock. The sheep bleated loudly, jumped, and scattered as Williams and White followed.

"You went too easy on him," growled Williams.

"You know what a Spanish war would do?" exclaimed Sharp. "We'd lose our cattle, maybe have our ranches burned. You want that?"

Slowing their mounts, the men rode back to Buzzard Roost Ranch.

"What are you going to do now?" asked Williams.

"I'll think of something," replied Sharp.

"You better make it fast," said Williams.

"Like I said, don't use violence or guns," said Sharp. "Let me think on it. It may not be right away, but trust me, I'll come up with some kind of solution."

***

Sharp was selling his horses as fast as they became rideable mounts. To improve his brood mares, Sharp went back to Missouri and, for $75 a piece, purchased a train car load of horses. While there, he got to thinking that his workers could use some Missouri mules to tend the fields. Stopping at a breeder's farm, he saw two large, feisty mules in a fenced pasture. They were running around chasing and harassing horses and burros.

"How much for those two?" asked Sharp.

"Mister," said the mule breeder, "I've got to tell you the truth; those mules are a pure consternation. They're ornery and chase everything in sight. I couldn't sell them to you. Why, they've jumped the fence and killed, I don't know how many sheep. They hate those critters, and I had to pay steep for the damage."

"Then why do you keep them?"

"Well, to be honest, they're plum mean to human and beast. But they've killed mountain lions, coyotes, and every varmint that came in their reach. They chased and took them critters in their teeth, threw them, and stomped them into the ground flatter than a pancake!"

"I'll take them," said Sharp.

"You can't say I didn't warn you. I'll sell 'em cheap and good riddance."

Altogether, Tom Sharp purchased six mules. He returned to Colorado with two car-loads of stock. Once there, he visited Williams and White.

"I want you to come see my two killer mules," said Sharp.

"What's that you say?" asked Williams.

"They're the meanest, orneriest, and toughest critters I ever encountered. The previous owner said they were hard on other creatures. I've given them both a separate stable and filled it with oats and corn to entice them to stay. I've got them locked in for now. I want you to come and help release them. We'll push them up on high country and see if what I've been told is true."

The three friends worked together to release the mules and chase them to higher graze. They pushed the big long-eared creatures exactly where Antonio Archuleta kept his sheep. True to the mule breeder's words, those two giant beasts tore into the sheep. They chased them in circles, biting and stomping and killing untold numbers. Then the mules ran to the tent where Archuleta was camping. Holding his staff, the sheepherder shouted bloody murder. The herder, with his dogs, ran up the mountain into ponderosa pines.

"I told you I would find a way," said Sharp.

"I'd laugh," said White, "but partner, I never seen such a gruesome sight. It got the job done, sure enough."

Chapter 19

"Killer mules!" said Williams grimly.

"I wouldn't have believed it if I hadn't seen it with my own eyes," commented White. "Whoever heard of such a thing?"

"Are we going to go after the mules?" asked Williams.

"I figure when they're done and get hungry, they'll come back to their stable," replied Sharp.

"If they don't?" asked White.

"Don't you think we already got our money's worth?" replied Sharp.

"They might return," said Williams, "if that Spanish herder doesn't shoot 'em first."

The mules returned to their makeshift stable and to the oats and corn. They were allowed to run loose, so they kept the sheep, coyotes, and other varmints away. After a few months of the mules roaming free-range, the stock was no longer being killed by predators. The mountain lions disappeared, chased clean out of the Huerfano River Valley, off mountain graze, and the dead line.

***

The three ranchers were together at Buzzard Roost Trading Post when Antonio Archuleta and a group of sheepherders paid a visit.

"Señor Sharp," said Archuleta. "Your mules, they chase and kill my sheep, my dogs, and bite my herders. They are crazy beasts. You must stop them."

"Didn't you say a few months ago that this was free graze country?"

"I did, but…"

"And, when I complained that your sheep were eating the grass down to the dirt, you shrugged your shoulders and said it was my problem. Or to that effect."

"But Señor Sharp, those mules, they are crazy."

"I told you, someday you would regret coming across the dead line," replied Sharp. "Everyone knows that was graze land for our cattle. Now keep your sheep on the other side of the dead line and away from those mules, and you'll do just fine."

"Señor, I want you to pay for…"

White and Williams put hands to pistol butts, and Tom Sharp stepped forward, bumping Archuleta off his front porch and down the steps. Tom's two friends followed.

"I used no violence against you, Archuleta," said Sharp. "Know this, if you harm those mules, you'll answer to me. If you come here and threaten us again, you'll regret it. You lost the confrontation you started. Accept it and go."

The group of angry sheepherders turned and walked away, muttering to each other in Spanish.

"Those mules were a Godsend," said Williams. "How did you ever find such creatures?"

"I told you I would solve our sheep and mountain lion problem," said Sharp, and he laughed. "To tell you the truth, it was pure luck. Let's go inside and have lunch."

CHAPTER 20

Chief Ouray and his band were still roaming southern Colorado from his summer camps on the Uncompahgre River, near Montrose, to the Huerfano River Valley in winter. It is said that, for a short time, he secured a 300-acre farm for his band on the Uncompahgre River. He irrigated farmland and grew crops for his tribe. Ouray stayed in a six-room furnished house that had a piano and China dishes. More unusual is that he became an Episcopalian and his wife, Chipeta, a member of the Methodist church. All this to gain acceptance from the whites.

Giving up the ranch, Chief Ouray and Chipeta returned to roaming with their tribe and doing their best to seek peace with the intruding whites. Over the years, Ouray visited Washington, DC, to meet Presidents Lincoln, Grant, and Hayes. Ouray, along with other Ute chiefs, signed treaties. Each time promises were not kept, and the treaties were broken.

Despite Chief Ouray's peace attempts with the whites, he refused to stop warring with the Arapaho and Apaches. The bloody conflicts between the tribes caused complaints from the settlers all across the Front Range. This stirred the US Army to take action. In 1867-68 they removed most of the Cheyenne and Arapaho to reservations; however, the Apaches and the Utes were still roaming free. Chief Ouray and his tribe were forced to a temporary reservation in the Los Pinos River area. In 1876, long before the final treaty of 1880, the southern band of Utes was moved west.

Acting after the fact, Tom Sharp and Raine tried to intervene. Together they wrote eloquent letters to the military, to politicians, and to the president. The response was always the same: "The settlers are afraid of the Utes, and they must be confined to reservations."

In an effort to help his friend, Tom Sharp gave funds and urged the government to build a house for Chief Ouray and his wife, Chipeta. The house was put on reservation land. Sharp traveled to visit the chief and found him living in a tipi.

"You come to see captured Indians?" asked Ouray.

"No, to see my friend."

"I have no friends," replied the chief. "I am now a tamed Indian. A wooden Indian without life. The kind that stands before your tobacco stores."

"Why don't you live in the house we built for you?"

"I don't want a house, Sharpy. I want my people's freedom."

"I tried, Chief. Raine, she tried. We wrote dozens of letters. I met with the military. We wrote to the president."

"And?"

"The same answer each time. The settlers coming west are afraid of free-roaming Utes."

"So you and your people lock us on a reservation? Take our freedom and take all our land and hunting grounds? I saw this day coming, and I learned all I could to prevent it. But you whites, you steal what is not yours. If we fight back, you kill or lock us up. Now our ways are gone forever, and you make me and my people like the living dead."

"I'm very sorry, chief."

"You say it, but you can never be more sorry than me. Once you were a friend to my people, so I will speak these words one-time to you and forever be silent."

"I'm listening," replied Sharp intently.

"When I became chief, I knew nothing. It was clear I must learn the white man's way. I did all I could to protect my people. I studied your ways; I went to Washington many times. Three presidents shook my hand, made promises, and signed treaties. Each time they were broken, and each time we lost more land and more freedom. You took it all. When you got it, you lock us up. We are like the garbage in the streets of your big cities, thrown away."

"What you say is true," said Sharp. "But, I also tried to protect you. I alone cannot fight a nation. I remain your friend, Chief Ouray. Once, you and your band saved my life. I tried to give you comfort with this house. It was the only thing left that I could think of to do for you."

"I have no friends. I will eat, sleep, and die in this tipi and never enter that government building. Go, Sharpy, I speak to you no more."

Tom Sharp rode back to Buzzard Roost Ranch: he had plenty of time to think along the way. Chief

Ouray and his band had been good friends. In fact, they had enriched him. It was the Utes who brought in the hides for trade. It was they who really found the Malachite copper and even, on occasion, solid chunks of silver. The conflict other whites had with the Utes was not an issue with the Sharp family. It was more than regrettable that he could not help his Indian friends. Sharp did not blame Chief Ouray for his contempt of all white men. After all, it was the end of their way of life.

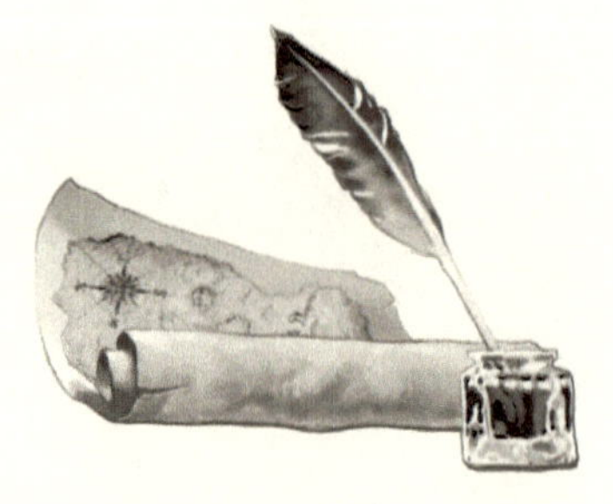

CHAPTER 21

With the Indians on the reservations, the Upper Huerfano River Valley citizens believed peace had finally come. But in Walsenburg, some twenty-eight miles from Buzzard Roost Ranch, a different kind of trouble was brewing for Raine, her son, Christopher, and the children who attended the Gardner school---trouble only Tom Sharp and his friends could solve.

***

Six years had passed since Big Jack Pepper got word that his wife Susan was dead. In all that time, Big Jack assumed his child had died with her. He had been told the Sharps took his wife to the trading post, and it was there she died. To this day, he resented the Sharps for interfering. Who did those fancy people think they were, getting involved?

In his own way, Pepper loved the woman he married. His continued drinking and violent behavior were partly due to his guilt over his wife's death. He knew he was responsible. During these years, Jack worked nights as an enforcer at the Alpine Saloon, a disreputable bar in Walsenburg. It was where thieves and criminals came for refuge, to drink, gamble, and find other pleasures.

The owner, Benny Strong, was a crook. He stole from his patrons and sold them homemade rotgut liquor. To keep order in the den of violent thieves, he hired the biggest, meanest man he could find, Big Jack Pepper, a fellow who didn't care whether he lived or died. Somehow, Strong was able to keep Big Jack in his employ.

"What are you going to do with him now, Benny?" asked Turner, the swamper.

The big enforcer sat passed out at a table in the saloon. The fellow had long dark hair, a large bushy beard and wore tattered clothing. He smelled bad and snored loudly. The big man sat in the midst of the dive that reeked of a mixture of alcohol, leftover smoke, kerosene lanterns, and vomit. The floor was littered with filled spittoons, peanut husks, and filthy sawdust.

"I don't know," said Benny. "I've never seen Big Jack this drunk before. Besides, it will take four men to pick him up and carry him to the back room."

"Well," said Turner, "if the regulars come in and see him this helpless, they'll kill him, sure."

"I know. I need to sober him up before tonight."

"Why do you keep him on?" asked the swamper.

"Because he's the one man that's big enough to keep this place together. You know the crowd who comes in here at night. Big Jack is the only one tougher than the rest of 'em. He doesn't care what happens to him in a fight, and they know it."

"Well then," said Turner. "I'll find two more men off the street to help us take him to his bed in the back. But you'll have to pay 'em."

Big Jack Pepper snored through the entire maneuver as four men lifted him out of the bar chair and carried him through the back to his room. In the process, a barrel of homemade whiskey was knocked over and rolled into a collection of bottles filled with the vile brew. Several of the bottles fell and broke. The smelly brown liquid spilled onto the rough board floor and slowly dissipated between cracks.

"Say!" yelled Benny. "That's good money you spilled!"

"We carried him," said one of the helpers. "Now pay up!"

"How about a glass of whiskey?" asked Benny.

"Not on your life!" said one of the men. "I ain't hankering to get poisoned. Turner promised us two bits each. Fork it over."

"Yeah, said the other helper. Hand it over."

"Four bits for a minute of work? Turner, you robbed me!"

"Better pay 'em," said Turner. "We couldn't have done it alone, and you couldn't leave Jack in that chair."

Benny grudgingly pulled out a change purse and picked out two 25-cent pieces.

"You fellows got the best of me today."

"First time for everything," laughed one of the men, and he pocketed the change.

His friend opened the saloon's back door, and the two stepped out into the alley.

"Ahh, fresh air," Turner and Benny heard the other fellow exclaim. "That place sure stinks."

"Better clean up the broken glass, Turner," said the saloon owner. "Once you get that done, gather some of those empty bottles behind the bar and bring them in here. Then find me a spout. You'll have to hustle to clean up the front. When you get done, come back and help me fill."

"Alright, boss," replied the swamper. "But I want a raise if I have to deal with Jack again. If it's your brew he got drunk on, I don't want to be around when he wakes up."

"Go on with you!" shouted Benny. "You just get your work done and keep your mouth off my business."

Big Jack Pepper lay on his bed in the back room of the saloon and snored his way through one whole night and day. When he awoke, he was weak, dizzy, suffering a severe headache, and every part of his body hurt. He stumbled out to the bar and leaned on it, his massive head down.

"Give me a beer and something to eat," said Jack in a raspy voice.

The bartender moved quickly, poured a beer, and then put together a sandwich. The big man gulped the mug of beer down, called for another, and nearly swallowed the sandwich whole. The man's breath was devastating, along with his body odor. Benny came into the saloon and saw the condition of his enforcer.

"Jack, glad to see you up. But you're a mess, and you smell worse. I'll have Harvey boil water and fix you a bath in the tin tub out back."

"What did you do to me?" roared the filthy man. "What kind of poison is that stuff you sell?"

"Hush, not here," said Benny, "go to the back."

Benny walked through the rear door of the saloon and called out to Harvey.

"Get that bath water ready!"

Big Jack stumbled to the tub, still holding his second beer mug.

"I told you not to drink my liquor," said Benny when Jack closed the door. "It's only for the customers. From now on, stick to the beer."

"I ought to wring your neck," replied Big Jack, "I feel like I been drugged and dragged down Main Street."

"Jack, it's your own fault. No one put that stuff down your throat except yourself. For two nights I've gone without your services. Last evening, towards midnight, a fight broke out, and if you noticed, the mirror's cracked, some lamps broke, and a couple tables and chairs are beyond repair. Lucky the place didn't burn down."

"Too bad it didn't," replied Big Jack.

"It took four of us to carry you to your bed," said Benny. "You would have burned up, along with the other buildings. Think on that."

"With that poison you sell, I wouldn't have known one way or the other."

"That's what you think? Jack, I provide you money, a place to sleep, girls on occasion, and that big horse you ride once in a while. And what do you do? Put on a big drunk and leave my place unguarded."

"I can't be workin' every night for you, Benny. Hire other men. I'm in no shape to work tonight."

"Jack, I may not be able to replace the likes of you, but you're still not irreplaceable."

"Whatever that means."

"What are you gonna do?"

"Benny, I'm going to get more food, something to drink, and lay down and sleep off this headache."

"Well, before you do, take that bath. Have Harvey trim your beard and cut your hair. You're beginning to look like a caveman."

Big Jack laughed, groaned, and touched his forehead with his free hand.

"Isn't that what you wanted?" asked Jack. "A caveman to keep the peace in this hell-hole?"

"Yes, but don't vex me. Go ahead, clean yourself up, take some aspirin powders, and then get some sleep. I expect you on duty by tonight."

"What you done to me, I ought to quit."

"Jack, with your reputation, no man is going to hire you or pay what I pay you. Go ahead, take the night off. Don't drink that rotgut I sell; stick to the beer. You do a good job around here, but don't push it."

"Whatever."

"Forgot to tell you, Jack. A weasely-looking little hombre came in last night while you were taking your siesta. He was asking about you."

"Wha'd he want," moaned Pepper, holding his head.

"Said you both worked for that hoity-toity Tom Sharp over in his stamping mill at Malachite. Something about the Sharps and your wife. Didn't know you had a woman, Jack!"

"Benny!" roared the big man, jumping up. "That's my business! Don't you never mention her again!"

"Suit yourself. No need to get riled."

Big Jack angrily threw his beer mug against a wall, and it exploded into fragments. He extended his arms, grabbed Benny's shirt front and vest, and lifted him forcefully from the ground. He held and shook the saloon owner as if he weighed nothing.

"You don't own me, Benny. Watch how you speak."

"Put me down, you fool. I'm the only friend you have in this town. Didn't I bail you out of jail and pay the lawyer? Haven't I helped you when no one else would? Don't bite the hand that feeds you. I've been trying to look out for you, but you make it mighty hard."

Big Jack set Benny on his feet and stepped back. "I reckon you've treated me better than most. But Benny, I won't be your man forever. Soon's I sober up, I'm figuring on..."

"Big Jack," said Benny. "You stay here. I'll raise your salary. I need you. In the meantime, take that bath, get cleaned up, and get some sleep. You'll see; it'll make you feel better."

"All right, Benny. But you be more careful about gettin' in my business."

"Sure, Jack," said the saloon owner. "But don't forget, I'm the best friend you got."

"Huh. If that were true, you would have paid me more a long time ago."

Big Jack Pepper took his bath, and the water turned black. So did the white towel the enormous fellow used to wipe dry. Changing into the clean underwear and clothes that Harvey provided, the barkeep trimmed the man's beard and hair. When finished, Harvey wakened Jack, and he stumbled back to his bedroom and slept the day and night through.

The next evening Big Jack was back at his perch, a podium with a chair. He wore a colt and a Bowie knife. Experience with law encouraged him to use a big club he held in his lap. Seeing the huge man, the rambunctious crowd kept their raucous behavior to an acceptable level.

Big Jack Pepper sat, and bar girls brought him food and drink through the night. There came a moment when the man had to relieve himself. He motioned for one of the barmen to come up and stand guard.

Going out back to a group of outhouses, Jack found an unoccupied one. He did his business and headed back to the saloon. Under dim lantern light, a man came forward.

"Mister Pepper," said the fellow.

"No one calls me that!" growled Jack. "Wha'd ya want?"

"You remember me? I'm Bill Watson. You and I used to search for copper up at Malachite. You know, for Captain Deus and Tom Sharp's stamping mill?"

Pepper stopped, squinted his eyes in the dim light, and looked down at the small fellow before him.

"Yeah? I don't remember much about them times. What you want?"

"Jack," said Bill. "I looked for you last night. Maybe you don't remember, but you helped me once. Someone told me you work here, so I came to tell you your son is alive."

"What?" roared Big Jack, bending down and putting huge hands on Bill Watson's shoulders. He squeezed. "What is that you say?"

"Ouch! If you'll stop, I'll tell you."

Jack let go, and the little man stepped back. Regaining his balance, he spoke out.

"I was pretty sure you didn't know. You have a son named Christopher."

"You lie!" roared Jack.

"I'm still working for the stamping mill in Malachite. Everyone up there knows about the boy. He's about so high and goes to the school in Gardner."

"WHERE IS HE NOW?" asked Big Jack in a stentorian voice.

"Mrs. Sharp took your wife in. She had her baby and died. An Indian woman named Raine is raising him."

"AN INDIAN!"

"Yes, she works at the Buzzard Roost and lives in a shack behind it."

"If you ain't tellin' the truth, I'll wring your neck. How's come you're telling me this?"

"I thought you ought to know. If I had a kid, I'd want to."

"Why wasn't I told before this?"

"Maybe folks were too scared to tell you?"

"And you ain't?"

"I told you, you did me a favor once. When I heard you worked here, I thought…"

Jack reached into a pants pocket and brought out three silver dollars. He held out a huge right hand towards Watson.

"Take them!" shouted Jack. "Now git!"

The little man took the coins, backed up, and quickly disappeared into the dark alley.

Overcome with emotion, Jack Pepper found a box behind the saloon and sat down. The wood creaked with the weight of the huge man. There Jack sat and thought. The longer he did that, the angrier he became.

Do I really have a kid? Thought Jack. *His name's Christopher? An Indian is raising him? A stinking no good... I hate this job, but how can I get money if I quit? I've got to...*

Big Jack Pepper rose to his feet and flexed his biceps and chest of hard muscle. The enormous six-foot, four-inch man clenched his fists with all his strength. His joints and sinews snapped with the tension and then released. He opened his mouth and roared loudly. "AWWWWW!" His mind was made up. All previous inhibitions and caution were thrown away. "I have a son!"

Jack turned and walked back into the bar. Patrons saw him coming, and those slow to get out of his way were roughly pushed aside. Big Jack walked to the other side of the saloon. Behind the stairs to the upper floor was the office door of Benny Strong.

This was the owner's private domain, and no one ever entered without knocking. Jack tried the handle, and the door was locked. Pushing hard with his shoulder, the wood in the door frame cracked from the enormous pressure. Backing up, he smashed the door frame to pieces. Benny Strong sat at a desk, two bright lanterns lighting the room. The forceful entrance shocked the owner. Benny bent down and opened a drawer to get at a pistol.

Jack flung himself across the desk and grabbed Benny by the throat. Sliding to his feet, Big Jack lifted the fellow by holding onto his neck.

"What...are...you...doing?" gasped Benny.

"Taking what's mine!" roared Jack, still holding Benny's neck.

Behind the saloon owner was a safe, and the door was open. Jack lifted the wheezing fellow higher by his neck. There was a snapping sound, and Benny lived no longer. The dead man fell to the floor. Jack found a satchel next to the desk. Picking up the leather bag, he opened it, and inside was coin and paper money. Opening the safe door wide, he saw a pile of greenbacks. The big man stuffed those in the satchel and came to his feet.

Some of the rougher men were near the broken office door peering in. Jack walked to the desk and saw the open drawer and the intricately engraved Colt pistol with ivory handles. He picked it up, opened the gate, and spun the cylinder. It was loaded. Holding the gun before him in his right hand and the satchel in his left, he walked out of the office and into the main part of the saloon. Jack lifted the colt and fired one round into the ceiling.

"I'm Jack Pepper, and I just took what was mine from that sneaky snake, Benny. I just quit. Take what you want. If any of you would like to ride with me, join me out back."

An enormous collective shout emitted from the crowd, and men stampeded for the bar. Jack walked steadily through the saloon and towards the back door. A burning lantern was hanging from a nail, and the big man picked it up and went outside. In the alley behind the outhouses was a small stable. Setting the satchel down, by lantern light, Jack gathered reins and bridle. Getting his horse to accept bit and bridle didn't take long. The man blanketed and saddled the mount and tightened the cinch. Picking up the leather satchel, he placed the handles over the pommel and led his animal into the alley. There, in the dim lantern light, stood five rough-looking men holding reins to their horses.

"You're that feller named Cy," said Jack to the largest of the outriders. "We were in jail together."

"Glad you remember, Jack," replied Cy. "Those three weeks we were together, I tried to get you to join us. That place in the mountains is doing great. We've rustled cattle and sheep. We're re-branding and have a big herd to sell."

"You're joining me?" asked Jack.

"Yeah, we need a big man like you. In jail, you didn't let anyone push you around. I liked that."

"I remember you telling me about that valley of yours. And I do need a place to hide out. I found out someone's got my boy. He's up in Gardner, and I'm going after him. Any objection to that?"

"One of my men was in the back alley. He heard a fellow tell you Tom Sharp and some Indian has your kid?"

"Yeah."

"When are you goin' for him?"

"Right now."

"We'll help you. It sounds like fun. That Sharp fellow did us a bad turn too."

The men mounted and rode towards Badito, Jack leading the way.

CHAPTER 22

Raine Stone found that after the Utes were forced onto reservations, her job at the trading post became immensely easier. Travelers were slow but steady, but nothing like trading with Indians. It was clear to her, that eventually, Buzzard Roost Trading Post would close. Still, she handled the accounting for the post, stamping mill, horses, and cattle. Raine drove Christopher, Crystal, and little Billy Sharp to and from school each day. On her days off, she helped the teacher, Aaron Wilburn.

On a Friday afternoon, six rough men galloped up to the schoolhouse and dismounted. Raine was there and, seeing the danger, she told the children to duck under their desks. The Indian woman joined Aaron Wilburn behind his desk, and they waited.

Big Jack Pepper ducked to enter through the front door. He stood, wearing a gun belt, the fancy colt in a leather holster. Some of the children whimpered in fear.

"I'm here for my son, Christopher Pepper," said Jack, his booming voice echoing through the large room.

"You are not allowed here, Jack Pepper!" Raine said, stepping around the desk.

The other five men stood in the doorway looking in. They laughed at the response from the woman.

"You're that Indian who's got my kid?" growled Big Jack.

"You abused your wife, Susan," said Raine. "She was left alone in a cold shack without food or water. It's been years. Christopher was never your child."

"I've killed men for saying less," bellowed Jack. "No Indian is going to give me a lecture."

Advancing, the big man went to grab Raine by the throat; instead, he got a kick to the groin. When he bent over in pain, she struck his neck with doubled fists. Jack collapsed. His men shouted foul oaths and ran into the schoolroom. One pulled a pistol and struck Raine's head. She fell onto the wooden floor, and blood pooled around her. A fifth man came through the front door carrying a canteen. He sprinkled water over Jack's face. Pepper awoke and gasped for air. Slowly, he rose to his feet. Looking down, he saw the Indian woman and the blood.

"Serves her right!" said Big Jack. "No Injun's gonna raise my kid! Where's my son?"

Jack's voice echoed against the four walls. The children cowered in fear, and some cried. The man looked directly at the school teacher. Aaron Wilburn backed up and hit the wall with a thud.

"Tell me where my son is, or so help me, you won't like what happens to you!"

"I…I…can't." gasped the teacher. "I have to protect…I would lose my job."

"You'll lose a lot more than that if you don't show me the boy!"

Jack's men laughed.

"That's Christopher," said a fearful little boy, pointing to where Christopher and Crystal knelt under a desk.

Jack walked over, grasped an arm, and dragged the boy out. He held him up to his face and snarled.

"Are you Christopher Pepper?"

"My name," said the boy, "is Christopher Stone. You're not my father. I've never seen you before."

"Your name ain't Stone and never will be, boy. You're my son. That Indian woman lied to you."

"Mama Raine doesn't lie," replied Christopher.

Big Jack shook the boy roughly in his huge mitts.

"I'll teach you manners! No kid of mine talks back."

"That's tellin' him," said one of the men.

"Come on," said Jack, holding the boy as if he were a flour sack. "Let's ride."

Big Jack Pepper went out the schoolhouse door first, carrying his son, and the five tough men followed. They went to their horses, and as quickly as they came, they were gone.

"Matthew," said the school teacher. "You shouldn't have told them."

"You're nothing but a stinking coward, Matthew Smith!" screamed Crystal Stone. "I'll never talk to you again as long as I live. You let them take my brother."

The other children, rising to their feet, murmured in agreement.

The teacher knelt beside Raine. Several children ran to the storage room for towels and a bucket of water. They returned, and a rag was wetted and applied to Raine's bleeding scalp.

"Will Mama be all right?" asked Crystal, holding onto her mother's arm.

The towel turned crimson. Wilburn applied more pressure and slowed the bleeding. Raine groaned and opened her eyes.

"Christopher?" she asked.

"Here," said Wilburn. "Let's get you onto a bench. I need to bandage your head."

Raine rose to her feet. The children put benches together, and the injured woman sat down. Wilburn ripped up a towel and tied a strip around Raine's wound. The bleeding slowed and stopped.

"They took him, didn't they?" said Raine.

"Yes, I'm sorry," replied Wilburn.

"Aaron," said Raine. "I'll stay with the children. You take my buggy, go to the trading post, and find Tom Sharp. Explain what happened. Tell him I'm going after my son, with or without him."

"Raine," said Wilburn. "You were unconscious, and you have a deep cut. You're…"

"Tell Sharp!"

The teacher did as asked. While he was gone, Raine went to the back room and cleaned her scalp, and applied a better bandage. Refusing the children's help, she went to her knees and mopped up her own blood.

"How can you fight those bad men, mama?" asked Crystal.

"Don't you worry, daughter," said Raine. "One way or the other, Christopher is coming home."

It took two hours, but Tom Sharp led John White, John Williams, and the German, Captain Deus, into the schoolyard. Wilburn followed in the buggy. White led two mules carrying supplies. Sharp had a saddled paint mustang for Raine and a rifle in a scabbard.

"It took you long enough," said Christopher's mother.

"I did my best," replied Sharp. "I knew I couldn't talk you out of going."

"The tracks show they vent toward the mountains," said Captain Deus. "Let's go."

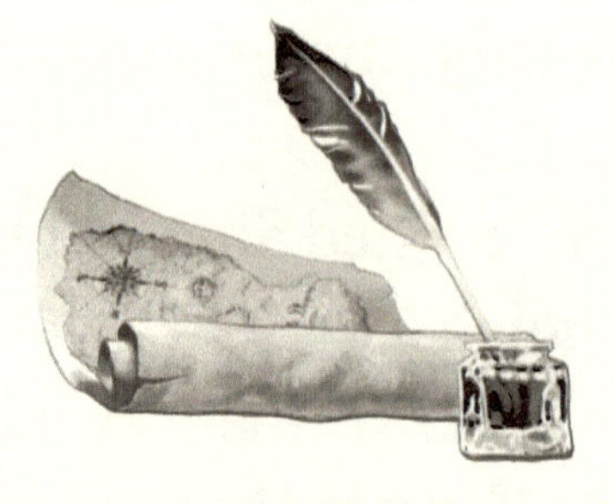

CHAPTER 23

Outside of the schoolhouse, Captain Deus located the tracks of the six kidnappers. Mounting his horse, the captain took the lead. The other four pursuers, with two pack horses, followed behind. The tracks led up a narrow road that passed Little Sheep and Big Sheep Mountains. Then they began to climb a steep trail below Iron Mountain.

Hitting a rocky area, Deus lost the hoof prints in a mix of wagon and horse tracks. Sharp dismounted and examined the trail. Finding fresh markings, he pulled his horse forward and slowly led the party up the mountain. It was Old Tex who taught Sharp his tracking skills, and he put them to good use. Raine dismounted, and when her boss lost sign, she was able to pick out distinguishing marks. It was slow going; halfway up the mountain, light began to fail and the trackers looked for a good place to camp for the night.

They picked a site next to a spring, enclosed by rock. It was sheltered enough to build a quick fire, heat coffee, and cook food. Bedrolls were laid out, and the large food panniers were suspended against predators. The pack animals were stripped of supplies and hobbled.

"We should have kept going," said Raine.

"And stumble in the dark?" replied Captain Deus.

"My son is with that monster and…"

"The captain is right, Raine," said Sharp. "We can't do anything in the dark. First light, and we'll be on their tracks."

"Where do you think they'll go?" asked White.

"In some hideout, no doubt," said Williams.

"This feller Pepper," said Captain Deus, "he vorks in that dirty saloon all those years and all of a sudden kidnaps Christopher. Vhy?"

"Someone must have told him about his son!" said White.

"Yes!" said Deus.

"I agree with the captain," said Sharp. "Big Jack finds out about his son and gets all worked up.

Somehow he joined with those others. I bet they have some hole-in-the-wall place."

"The whole bunch of them looked like thieves and rustlers," said Raine. "Five bearded fellows as tough as Pepper. If he's done anything to hurt Christopher, I'll…"

"He von't hurt dat boy," said Captain Deus. "He might be rough on him, but he vill do no real harm. You vill nicht worry, please."

"Pepper's such a big hairy beast," said Raine. "He's like a grizzly, only worse."

"Huh," exclaimed Williams.

"I'm confident we'll find them tomorrow," said Sharp.

"We have to," said Raine. "And I'll be the one who gets Christopher."

The fire was out, and a cool wind blew. As if by signal, everyone went to their bedrolls except the woman. She had a headache, and the wound on her forehead bothered her. She removed the bandage and threw the blood-soaked cloth into the cold fire pit. Taking some plants gathered along the trail, she mashed them on stone and made a poultice. Using a strip of cloth, Raine applied the concoction and tied it tightly around her head.

Taking a drink from a canteen, Raine swallowed aspirin powder. Sitting, she could not help but worry over her adoptive son. She loved Christopher every bit as much as her own daughter. Hadn't she saved his life and cared for him all these years? He was such a clever and kind boy. Nothing like his father.

Looking up at the night sky, she saw a half-moon rising above the ponderosa pines and stone crags on the mountain. In the distance, coyote packs in various locations began their ferocious high-pitched wailing, calling back and forth to each other in their nightly hunt. Crickets chirped, and around the water, small frogs croaked. The wind increased, and the limbs in the trees rubbed against each other, making a constant rustling sound. Several owls hooted in the distance; far away, a long lonely howl of a wolf echoed across the mountain land.

Raine was up before dawn. Knowing men, she wanted no delay. She made a fire, cooked bacon and eggs, cut portions of bread, made coffee, and laid out utensils, plates, and cups. She carefully extinguished the fire, then, just before first light, she woke the four by shaking their shoulders.

No conversation was necessary and the men got up, ate, and drank their coffee. White and Williams gathered the horses and each man saddled his own. Raine assisted with the hobbles and loading the pack mules.

The wind from the night before further blurred the tracks. Carefully following the kidnappers' imprints, it took until the afternoon before Sharp and Raine discovered them leaving the main trail. After that, tracking was easier. At four in the afternoon, they came across sheep grazing. The party found a trail leading to granite dikes rising high into the air.

"There's a guard up on the cliff!" exclaimed Raine. "Get into the trees."

The group dismounted and hid their animals in the dense woods.

"Now vhat?" whispered the former German captain. "Like Tom Sharp say. Hole in vall."

"So you know, you're a legally deputized posse," said Sharp. "Something I arranged with Sheriff Sproull in Walsenburg."

"Now he tells us," said White.

"It's a new arrangement. I fixed it up with the sheriff after that sheepherder trouble."

"Goot to know," said Deus.

"How do we know that guard over yonder belongs to the kidnappers?" asked Williams.

"Sharp and I will climb the mountain," said Raine. "We'll find a way."

The other men turned to Sharp.

"What she said," replied the leader.

CHAPTER 24

It was Raine who led the way through the trees, circling where the guard now sat on a granite rock. The Ute woman came to the dike and found a place to climb. Hidden from the guard's view, Sharp and Raine reached the top. Both were able to look down into the canyon. There was a grass-filled valley below. In the distance, sunlight reflected off water, and around the pond, a few head of cattle and sheep grazed. A log cabin built in the middle of the green pasture contained corrals and in them, a number of horses. Smoke rose from a chimney, and a man was on one side of the building, axe in hand, chopping wood.

"I can't tell if it's them," said Raine, disappointed.

Tom Sharp produced a small spyglass. He extended it and put it to one eye. After a time,

he handed it to Raine. She looked through it and studied the man with the axe.

"I'm still not certain."

"They aren't going anywhere," said Sharp. "We followed their tracks. They have a guard. This is an outlaw setup if I ever saw one. It's them, Raine."

"How can you be so certain?"

"Deduction. Have faith. We'll sit and wait until we know for sure."

"Then what? How will we ever get close enough to…"

"The obvious," said Sharp. "We'll camp and wait until past midnight. In the dark, we'll take care of the guard and walk across the pasture until we get to the cabin. Then one of us will sneak in and take your son."

They sat patiently and occasionally scoped the valley. Sharp worried about what the rest of the posse would do. He climbed down, returned to the camp, and told them they wouldn't make a move until after midnight. Taking his time, Sharp joined Raine at the top of the cliff. There was an outhouse near the cabin. Through the collapsible telescope, Raine saw Big Jack Pepper come out of the cabin. As she watched, Christopher came through the door and walked alone to the little building. Sharp could tell who they were with his naked eye.

Now, thought Raine, *we are certain.*

After a time, the boy came from the outhouse and stood motionless. Looking at the canyon entrance, the child made a decision and started to run toward it. It was a long distance away. Raine watched and then heard the loud voice of the big man echo across the valley. Christopher did not stop. He kept running, heading for the entrance.

"That's my boy," whispered Raine proudly.

Despite repeated angry calls from Big Jack, the boy kept going. Watching anxiously, Raine saw the guard appear before the narrow entrance, rifle in hand. He stopped the boy's escape. Big Jack Pepper was now riding a horse bareback toward the child. He rode close, angrily reached down, jerked the boy up in front of him, and returned to the corrals. Raine watched helplessly as the angry man dragged her son back into the cabin.

"Don't worry, we'll get Christopher," whispered Sharp. "For sure, sometime after midnight, we'll go get him."

"What happens if it goes badly?"

"No matter what, we'll get him."

"He's such a good boy, Tom," said Raine. "I just can't lose him. This isn't fair."

"I think both of us realized long ago that nothing in this world is really fair," said Tom. "But that doesn't mean we don't keep trying to make it better for those we love."

"Yes, for those we love," replied Raine.

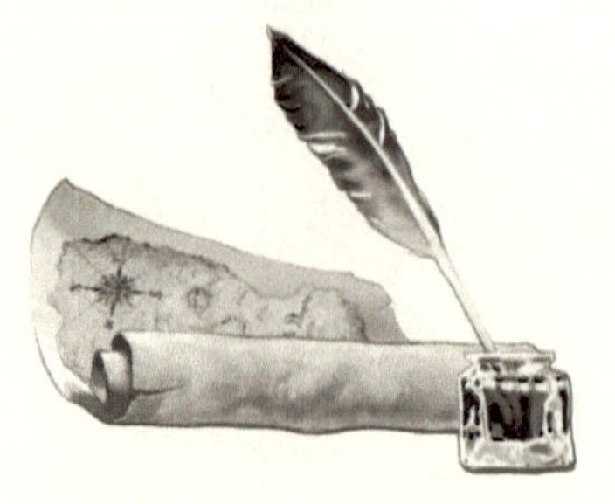

CHAPTER 25

Raine led the way down off the mountain cliff, and Sharp followed. The posse sat on rocks and a fallen log and waited. They had a cold camp and chewed on bread, cheese, and jerky, and drank water. Time moved slowly; it seemed like it took forever for daylight to wane. Toward dusk, they began a whispered conversation.

"We'll try to take the guard alive if we can," said Sharp.

"How will we do that?" asked Williams.

"At dark, Raine will go up to the perch to watch. If sometime between then and after midnight, they change guards, we'll try to grab the new one."

"And vhen we approach, vhat ist your plan?" asked Captain Deus.

"Once we get the guard, we'll sneak in and surround the cabin," said Sharp.

"And then?" asked White.

"We hope they'll be asleep, and one of us goes in and rescues the boy."

"That will be me," said Raine.

"And venn it goes schrectlich, I mean terrible, vhat then?" asked the German.

"I don't think anyone of us will not do what we can to save Christopher. If shooting starts, we watch where our bullets go. Don't hit the boy, but we defend ourselves as best we can."

"Doesn't sound like much of a plan," said Williams.

"If any of you have a better one," said Sharp, "tell me."

"It's times like these," said John White, "when I wish I was back with my wife."

"Me, too," said Williams.

"Ahh," commented the former German captain. "You boys live a gentle life. Fighting is the ultimate contest."

"We are doing what we have to," said Sharp. "But we must be careful."

Not a word was spoken for a long while.

"Raine," said Deus, breaking the silence, "Vhat are you going to do after we get your boy?"

"Now, it's probably not the time to say it, but my dream is to have a ranch."

"You would quit your job?" asked Sharp.

"No, I would still work for you," replied Raine. "I believe a ranch would keep my children safe. Would you help me, Tom?"

"I vill not live forever," said Deus. "I sell you 160 acres. Land I purchase near Malachite and along the Huerfano River. Plenty of grass and water for cattle, but I cannot give it away."

"I'm surprised, Raine," said Sharp. "If this is what you want, once we get your boy, I'll help you."

Darkness fell over the land, and Raine quietly slipped away and climbed up to her hidden spot on the granite dike. Stars began to appear and shine brightly. A half-moon was already up and illuminating the ground. Dark shadows spread across the canyon. It was easy to see the meadow below and the distant cabin in the bright moonlight. A light breeze blew, crickets chirped all around, and animals hunted in the night. It was a balmy, quiet place to watch and think.

I must get Christopher safely. I must. Tom's plan has to work.

Far below, the cabin door opened and yellow light flooded across the yard. A man came out, closed the door, and stood looking up at the sky above. He was holding a rifle, then turned and began walking toward the canyon entrance. This was the changing of guards. Raine hurried down the dark pathway. One time she skidded and hit her injured forehead on a rock. She could feel blood dripping down her face but paid no attention. Once on flat ground, she ran through the trees, putting her hands before her. She was whipped and smacked by low limbs and brush but pushed through to the camp.

"A guard is coming," whispered Raine to the group.

"You're hurt," said Tom Sharp, seeing the blood on her face under the bright star and moonlight.

"It is nothing. Hurry, we must..."

Sharp signaled, and the five moved quietly to the valley entrance. They saw the first guard climb down from the rocks and approach the new guard, on flat open ground. The posse hurried to the trail the guard had just left. They hid and waited. In the silence of the night, they heard every word the outlaws exchanged.

"See anything?"

"Nawww."

"I don't see why Big Jack makes us do this. No one will find us out here."

"Better do what he says. Hate to be on the other side of those fists of his."

"Yeah, you're right. It's a shame the way he treats that little boy."

"If he keeps at it, that lad is going to grow up to be one tough hombre."

"Huh! Just like his old man!"

"Good luck, Frank."

"Happy dreams, Shorty."

The five waited, and the guard came to the trail and took his time climbing. It was Raine who came up from behind and, with great force, struck the man on the back of his head with the stock of a Winchester rifle. The guard fell, and within moments the fellow was bound and gagged.

"You hit him hart," said the German.

"Yes," said Raine, "I did."

They carried the guard through the woods and back to their cold camp. Taking no chances, more rope was used, and the fellow was tied securely to a tree, unconscious and sitting up. Raine found a canteen and cloth and cleaned her wound. Then she took a drink. The party waited anxiously. Raine paced, and the other four sat on rocks and waited. Hours past midnight, Sharp pulled a watch and, in the light from above, examined the face. It was late. The leader of the posse stood up.

"It's past three. If the rest of them are not asleep by now, they never will be. Let's go."

Crossing through the pass and into the canyon took longer than they thought. The walk seemed interminable. At the cabin, Sharp signaled, Williams went to the left side, White to the right, and Captain Deus took the rear as planned. Tom Sharp seized Raine hard by the shoulders and whispered in her ear.

"Let me go inside. A pistol works better than a rifle. Let me grab the boy and…"

"But it is my…"

"Raine, please. Christopher knows me. When I wake him, he'll do what I say."

"He may be tied," said Raine, and handed her boss a small sharp jackknife she always carried in her pocket.

Tom Sharp grasped the latch, raised it slowly, and cautiously began to open the door. Raine watched, her rifle at the ready. There was a long slow screech as the door opened wide. It was dark inside, but not totally. Star and moonlight illuminated part of the entrance. One window let in light, enough to see by. Still, Sharp stood quietly and did not move. Then he took two steps inside and waited for his eyes to adjust to the gloom.

After a few minutes, he began to slowly inch forward. The place smelled of stale tobacco smoke, cooking, and unwashed bodies. Loud snoring erupted from men on bunks. Raine peered inside, and her heart beat rapidly as she watched her boss advance.

Sharp moved forward, counting the snoring men as they slept. There were four of them. He passed through the open cabin to the far wall. There was a door leading to another room. Gently, cautiously, the man lifted the latch and began to push, the door creaked loudly, and he stopped. Inch by inch, creak by creak, Sharp continued. Big Jack slept in a large bed, snoring loudly. He sounded like a grizzly asleep in his den, and the noise was deafening. Sharp stepped inside, and a floorboard squeaked. The snoring stopped. Holding his breath, pistol in hand, moon and starlight gleamed off the metal. The snoring started, stopped, and with loud staggered spurts, returned to a steady rhythm.

Looking down, Tom Sharp saw Christopher lying at the foot of the bed. Just like Rain said, there was a rope tied to a bedpost, and it led to the boy's feet. There were innumerable strands tied around the boy's lower legs. Sharp slid his pistol into his holster. With a quick movement, he knelt down and firmly placed one hand over the boy's mouth and the other on his forehead to hold the child down. The boy's eyes opened, and he fought to be free. His rescuer whispered close to the boy's ear.

"It's your friend, Tom Sharp. Your mother's outside. Quiet now. I'll untie you. Let me carry you out."

The boy looked up, trying to see. His eyes were big and round. Sharp could see bruises on the boy's face even in the moonlight.

"Nod, if you understand," whispered Sharp.

Big-eyed, the boy lay frozen and then, comprehending, nodded his head furiously. Sharp grabbed the knife, opened a blade, and cut at the ropes. It took some effort to saw through the hemp. Once cut, he folded the knife and dropped it in a pocket. Putting strong hands around the boy's back and under his legs, he lifted him. Big Jack lay in his bunk, snorting and snoring.

Carefully, the rescuer stepped forward, and once again, the board squeaked. This time even louder. Big Jack Pepper's snoring stopped.

"What's going on?" grumbled the man.

Taking no chances, Sharp held the boy tightly and ran through the cabin. He hurried past the other four outlaws, through the open door, and outside. Behind came the roar of Big Jack Pepper.

"They've got my boy!" roared the outlaw.

A pistol was produced from somewhere, and Big Jack fired it into the roof.

"Wake up, you fools!" he shouted. "Get that fellow."

Raine stood beside the open cabin door and peered in. She saw the flash of the revolver and Big Jack moving toward her. With the loud gunshot, two of the five men slid from their bunks and onto the floor. Jack got tangled up with one and fell. His pistol discharged, and the bullet struck Raine in her leg.

The woman fell, and on the way down, she pointed her rifle and fired. She saw the effect of the bullet as she hit the ground. Big Jack Pepper, rising to his feet, froze, struck in the head, he slowly began to fall backward and hit the cabin floor. The remaining four men shouted in fear, and one kept repeating.

"Don't shoot, don't shoot!"

"We give up!" shouted another.

Sharp, holding Christopher, continued running out onto the open valley and waited. He watched Williams, Deus, and White race past Raine and into the cabin. One of them fired a shot into the air and then shouted orders.

"Out with you," exclaimed White. "If you want to live, get into the yard!"

Under star and moonlight, Sharp clearly saw his posse push the four remaining outlaws out of the cabin. The tough men were in various stages of dress, and each had his hands and arms raised high into the air. Still, Sharp waited, holding the boy until two lanterns were lit and rope was found. The hands and feet of the four kidnappers were tied securely.

The boy was put down, and he saw Raine.

"Ma-ma!" he shouted, running to his mother, who sat with her back against the outside wall of the cabin. "Oh, Ma-ma, you're hurt!"

"Christopher," called Raine, giving her son a big hug. "This is nothing. Just a scratch. In a few weeks, I'll be good as new. But look at you! My brave boy. Did those bad men hurt you?"

"The big one did, Mommy. He told me he was my father."

"You never mind. You're safe now."

"Is…is that bad man dead, Mommy?"

"Christopher," replied Raine, "I promise he will never hurt you again."

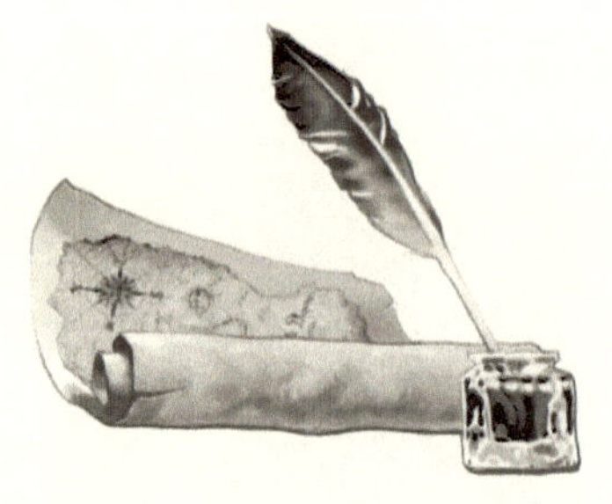

CHAPTER 26

The posse's last act before leaving was to shove the sheep out of the valley and barricade the entrance. They left the stolen cattle to fend for themselves. Someday they would return to deal with those that were branded and herd them back to their rightful owners.

It was early dawn as the group rode back toward Captain Deus's ranch. Christopher sat in front of Raine, and the two talked and hugged often. Sharp, Deus, White, and Williams guarded and pushed the five captured outlaws forward down the trail. Attached to the pommel of Sharp's saddle was a heavy leather satchel. Papers inside the bag revealed the stolen money that belonged to Benny Strong at the Alpine Saloon. When asked, one of the outlaws said Pepper killed the saloon owner. The rescuers were aware of the money. None counted it but knew it was thousands of dollars.

The posse discussed what to do with the stolen loot. By the time they stopped for a meal, the men had come to an agreement. The entire group dismounted and had jerky and water.

It was a long ride down the mountain pass, and just before dark, they came to Captain Deus's ranch. There they stopped to water the horses. The five prisoners were secured, then Deus approached Christopher's mother.

"Raine," said the captain. "Vee vould like to speak to you of matters of importance. Sharp vill explain."

"When John Williams was bandaging your wound, I went back into the cabin," said Sharp. "I checked to make sure Pepper was dead, and I left him on the cabin floor. I searched the first room and made a bundle of weapons. No reason to leave them behind. But in Pepper's room, I searched further and found a satchel of money. It was thousands in gold, silver, and paper. The money belonged to Benny Strong. The fellow that owned the Alpine Saloon."

"Yes?" said Raine.

"You said you vanted a ranch," responded Captain Deus. "Vell, I take the price for 160 acres from the money bag and give you deed to the land."

Raine, pulling on the bandage, looked up at Deus. She stopped fidgeting and just stared.

"Mommy!" exclaimed Chris, sitting by his mother. "We're going to have a ranch!"

The makeshift posse moved closer.

"And horses and cattle!" said Williams. "I will take the cost of five horses and five steers from the money."

"And I and Sharp will do the same," said White.

"Am I to start my ranch on stolen money?" asked Raine. "Is that legal?"

"Legal enough," explained Sharp. "There are thousands of dollars here, earned by a crooked saloon owner and taken by his own employee."

"Ve take out money for building," said Deus. "Vhat we take ist very small. Call it your revard money for catching outlaws."

"We give the rest to the sheriff," said White.

"Yes," replied Captain Deus. "They vill tell our story and everyone vill know Big Jack Pepper is dead. To keep you safe, ve say ve killed him."

"You will build us a cabin?" asked Raine.

"Captain Deus will find workman and send for supplies," said Williams.

"I bet you'll be moving in before winter," explained Sharp.

"I don't know what to say," replied Raine.

"Say thank you, Mommy," exclaimed Chris.

At that, the men laughed, and eventually, Raine joined in.

"This will be my children's legacy. And I thank you."

"It vas you, who did in Jack Pepper," said Deus. "He was a bad man. Strange fate, but from him you get your revord."

Captain Deus remained at his ranch. The remainder of the posse and the prisoners rode on to Buzzard Roost Trading Post. When they reached their destination, Katherine Sharp met her husband. Raine's little girl, Crystal, ran to greet her mother and her brother. Relieved, the weary party rested. They tied and locked up the prisoners, had a late dinner, and slept the night.

Sharp, White, and Williams escorted the five kidnappers to Walsenburg and the Sheriff in the morning. The money was handed over within the hour, and everyone in Walsenburg knew their story.

It took time, but Sharp made sure the kidnappers were prosecuted. They were convicted and sent to jail at the Territorial Correctional Facility, Canon City.

BUZZARD ROOST
TRADING POST

CHAPTER 27

With the capture of the outlaws, a steady routine returned to the residents of Huerfano Valley. As promised, work began on Raine's ranch, corrals were put up, and foundations for the barn and cabin began.

Tom Sharp once again became very involved in his businesses. He spent hours away from his family. One evening as Tom, Katherine, and the children sat on the front porch, enjoying the cool evening breeze and listening to the loud buzz of the cicadas, Billy made a request.

"Papa," said the child, "you promised to take me fishing. Can we go tomorrow?"

Tom shook his head and scowled.

"I'm sorry, son. I have buyers coming in the morning to look at our horses."

"What about after they leave?" Continued the boy.

"Not then, either. It will have to be another day. Pedro is going to help me measure for a new corral."

Billy sat on the lower step, biting his bottom lip, trying not to cry.

"It's time for bed, children," said their mother. "Tell your father good night."

Billy and Elizabeth kissed Tom's cheek as Katherine held baby Emma for Tom to hug.

Soon Mrs. Sharp returned and sat beside her husband. She let it be known that she wanted his undivided attention.

"Tom, we are blessed."

"Yes, dear, we are," replied Sharp.

"You kept your promise to me," said Katherine. "Our children, our friends, and their families are prospering. We are so lucky. We have a school, the trading post still has customers, and the horse and cattle sales continue."

"Yes?" asked Sharp. "You can't fool me, Katherine. Not after all this time. What are you leading up to?"

"You've fulfilled your promise, Mister Sharp, but the children and I want more from you."

"More?" said Tom, his mouth open in astonishment. "Katherine. This doesn't sound like…"

"You gallivant across the country, helping others while abandoning me and the children. It has to stop! Why do you think I started those Friday dinners? To keep you home!"

"Gallivant? Abandon?"

"Exactly. And so help me, Tom Sharp, I've had enough of it. Either you spend more time with us, especially at night, and pay attention to Bill, Elizabeth, and Emma or…"

"Or what, Katherine?"

"Or I take the children and return to Marion County, Missouri, and my parents. Then you'll know what it's like to be left alone all the time."

"You wouldn't!"

"Oh, wouldn't I? Remember how you returned to court me and how angry I was? Well…I am once again in that state. You must promise to do less with business and your friends. You must stop going around saving others and start spending more time with your family, or…"

"You leave to your parents?"

"Precisely!" responded Katherine in a clear firm voice.

"How long have you been feeling this way?" asked Tom.

"Ever since Emma was born, it's been building. After the children came, I thought you would settle down and pay more attention to us. But recently, it's getting worse. You travel the country purchasing horses, supplies, and cattle, and every year you go to Denver to the Colorado State Fair to run the horse department. Then you joined the Masons clear to Walsenburg."

"Not everyone can become a Third-Degree Mason," spoke up Tom.

"And those horses of yours! That $1400 Cleveland Bay from England and that $1800 Francois trotter from France…"

"What about them?"

"Why, you spend more time and money on them and speak more about those animals than you do your own children!"

"That's unfair, Katherine. Don't you see it's to improve the ranch? And the contacts I make help me sell our better breed of horses and for a good price."

"That's not all, Tom. You volunteer time to the sheriff, chase outlaws, and unnecessarily put your life at risk. It's almost as if you're finding ways not to stay at..."

"I didn't know you felt this way about it. I thought I was doing what was necessary for the community."

"Yes, but what about your own family? Doing what is necessary for Bill, Elizabeth, and Emma? They hardly ever see you or spend time with you."

"Not true. Didn't I take Bill to sit on Chief Ouray's knee when he was young? Don't we have the neighbors over?"

"Yes, but hardly enough. Sometimes, we barely see you."

"Well…what do you want from me then, woman?"

"Woman, is it? Tom Sharp, either you give your promise to stay at home nights and spend more time with the children, or so help me..."

"Yes?"

"We'll leave."

"Don't I provide for you, Katherine? Haven't you had every good thing money can buy? Didn't I keep my promise?"

"Yes, you have. But money isn't everything, Tom. If you go on this way, your children won't even know you."

"I suppose..."

"You suppose? Either you give your promise and keep it, or..."

"Katherine, I can't just stop. I have responsibilities to others, to the ranch, and to the businesses. I can't just stay home, or it will all fall apart."

"Then make us a part of it."

"How?"

"When you go on a business trip, take us with you. If I or the children can't stay with you while you do work, hire someone else to do it, and spend more time with us."

"I probably...could do that. But don't you see, by asking me to make this change, you are taking away who I am and how I have lived all these years? Do you really want me to do that?"

"Yes!" exclaimed Katherine in great heat.

"I see you're serious," said Tom, rising to his feet.

"You better take me seriously."

"All right, I will do as you say."

"You promise?"

"I do."

"Husband," smiled Katherine. "I've never known you to break your word. Not to me or anyone. I am so glad we had this little talk."

Katherine rose and stood before her man. She looked him straight in his eyes, came close, hugged him, and kissed him seductively. Once again, Sharp held his mouth open in surprise. And then, slowly, he began to laugh.

"Katherine, you played me."

"Well…perhaps just a little bit."

Tom put his arms around his wife, hugged and kissed her, and then continued to chuckle. Eventually, Katherine joined in.

The next morning, Katherine awoke with renewed exuberance over making up with her husband. What happened the night before filled her with excess energy. She went about breastfeeding Emma and then woke Elizabeth and Bill to get up, wash and dress. Fixing an ample breakfast, she awakened her husband, and by the time he came to the table, a hearty breakfast was before him.

"You seem to be in a good mood, Kate," said her husband, sounding in an equal frame of mind.

"I'm happy, Tom," said Katherine. "I'm so glad we worked out our differences. I am sure you will be with us and closer to the family from now on."

"I'm glad it's settled, too, honey. After all, I am just as committed as you. I wouldn't ever do anything to deliberately set us apart."

"Good," smiled Katherine. "This morning, I've arranged for the new housekeeper to watch Emma and Elizabeth while Raine and I take the children to school. Yesterday, Raine took the funds from the safe. You know, for renovations and the new stove for the schoolhouse. She gave the money to the teacher. It had to be there for the workman coming at eight o'clock sharp."

"You must be proud, Katherine. You and Raine worked so hard to raise the money."

"Yes, we are. Our bake sales and monthly dances paid off."

After breakfast, the housekeeper came to clean up. Tom went into the store to stock shelves and take inventory while Katherine had the liveryman harness the buggy. Raine and her children came from the cabin, and they all crowded into the small vehicle for the short ride to the school.

Raine got out first, and the children followed. Katherine stayed behind to secure the conveyance. When she finally entered the building, she saw the front door was cracked and damaged. The teacher, Aaron Wilburn, in great distress, was talking to Raine.

"I'm so sorry," said Aaron, turning to Katherine. "I left the money hidden in a box in the bottom drawer. I knew something was wrong when I came this morning, and the front door was broken open."

"But how did they know about the money?" asked Katherine.

"Obviously, someone saw us take it from the safe," said Raine. "Someone must be…"

"The new housekeeper!" said Katherine. "And I left the babies in her care. Raine! Come with me! Aaron, watch the children! We'll tell my husband, and then we'll be back with money to pay the workman."

Raine helped untie the buggy, and both jumped aboard. Katherine drove fast and furiously.

"We don't know it was the housekeeper," said Raine.

"Who else could it be?" shouted Katherine. "Everyone else has been with us for years!"

Arriving at Buzzard Roost, both women got out of the buggy. Raine stayed by the vehicle and waited while Katherine raced to her husband.

"Tom!" she shouted as she entered the store, "the schoolhouse was broken into and the money stolen!"

Tom came forward and, seeing his wife in an agitated state, put his arm around her.

"Take a moment," said Tom. "Collect your thoughts and tell me what happened."

Katherine took a deep breath and explained what she saw and suspected.

"If you think it was the new housekeeper," said Tom, "you no longer have to worry. A man I didn't know came to the post and asked for her. Then she spoke to me, said it was an emergency and quit."

"So it was her. I bet that man was one of the thieves."

"It looks that way," said Sharp. "Now, tell me exactly what you want me to do."

"Raine and I worked so hard to earn that money. It took an entire year. And those thieves broke down the door of the schoolhouse. I'm asking to borrow money from you, Tom, to pay for the stove and workman until. . ."

"Until what?"

"Until you track down those thieves and get our money back!"

Taking money from a change box hidden under the counter, Tom counted out the needed sum and handed it to Katherine.

"Here," he said. "But what about what you said last night? That I should stay home and leave it to the sheriff."

"It would take too much time, and the thieves might get away!"

"All right, if that's what you want, I'll gather a posse and supplies, but no telling how long we will be gone. And again, you insisted…"

"Tom Sharp! Forget everything I said last evening. We can't allow thieves to steal from schoolchildren."

Katherine helped Tom gather provisions and together they went to the stable where he saddled and mounted his thoroughbred.

"My love," she ordered, pointing into the distance. "I don't care how long it takes or what you must do, but don't stop until you find those crooks!"

Tom Sharp spurred his horse and smiled to himself as he rode away.

CITED RESEARCH SOURCES FOR TOM SHARP

Books

Ralph C. Taylor, "Colorado *South of the Border*" Tom Sharp Settled Buzzard's Roost, in Huerfano Ute Land. 1st ed., Sage Books, 1963, pp 144-150.

Stephen E. Ambrose, "*Nothing Like It In the World: The Men Who Built the Transcontinental Railroad 1863-1869.*" 1st ed., Simon & Schuster, 2001

Web Pages

Mrs. Lida A. Meyer. "*Tom Sharp's Post.*" "*History of Upper Huerfano Valley, Interview with William (Bill) P. Sharp, by Jeannette Thach.*"

"Tales About Tom Sharp, Compiled By Agnes Wright Spring." "Colorado Magazine." Vol 38, no. 1, January 1961 pp. 19-41. https://www.historycolorado.org/sites/default/files/media/document/2018/ColoradoMagazine_v38n1_January1961.pdf

Mary Richardson, Profile Manager. "*Welcome to Huerfano County, Colorado History.*" History Timeline. https://www.wikitree.com/wiki/Space:Huerfano_County%2C_Colorado

"*Act for the Government and Protection of Indians.*" The Gold Rush | Article https://www.pbs.org/wgbh/americanexperience/features/goldrush-act-for-government-and-protection-of-indians/

1861 Map of the United States showing territories. National Geographic Map: file:///home/t-1/Desktop/1861%20National%20Geographic,%20%20Use%20this%20one.%20%20Boundary%20Between%20the%20United%20States%20and%20the%20Confederacy.html

1867 Map of the United States showing Dakota Territory encompassing Cheyenne. David Rumsey Map Collection. https://www.

davidrumsey.com/luna/servlet/detail/RUMSEY~8~1~2217~170048:Map-of-the-United-States-and-Territ

1867 photo of Cheyenne, Dakota Territory. University of Wyoming. https://www.wyominghistoryday.org/theme-topics/collections/items/cheyenne-dakota-territory-1867

ADDITIONAL SOURCES FOR CALIFORNIA HISTORY

Gold, Greed and Genocide, Unmasking the Myth of the 49ers, Project, Pratap Chatterjee Underground pamphlet, (1998)

Rooted in Barbarous Soil: People, Culture, and Community in Gold Rush California. Starr, Kevin and Orsi, Richard J., Editors, University of California Press. (2000)

California: A History. (Modern Library Chronicles) Kevin Starr, Random House (2005)

The Destruction of California Indians. University of Nebraska Press, Robert F. Heizer, (1974)

Genocide in Northwestern California: When our world cried. Indian Historian Press, Jack

Norton (1979) *The California Indians: A Source Book.* Robert F. Heizer (Editor) M. A. Whipple (Editor) (1971)

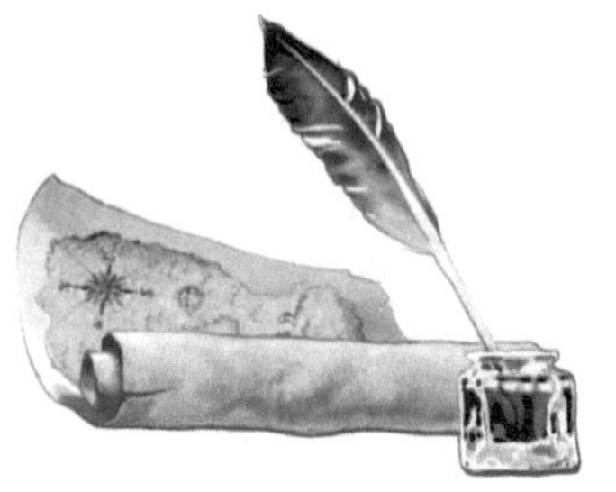

ABOUT THE AUTHOR

Charlie Steel is a novelist and internationally published short story writer.

Steel, author of **Desert Heat, Desert Cold and Other Tales of the West,** and other novels and anthologies, has worked in assorted occupations starting at the age of ten. Some of his experiences include service in the Army, laborer in the oil fields, construction, foundry worker, and salvage diver. Early in his life, he was recruited by the US Government and spent seven years behind the Iron Curtain. His undercover assignments monitored Russian activity.

Steel attended eight universities and currently holds five degrees, including a PhD.

Charlie Steel is an avid traveler, hunter and fisherman. He lives on an isolated ranch at the base of Greenhorn Mountain in Southern Colorado. (www.charliesteel.net)

ABOUT ILLUSTRATOR

Illustrator Barabash Sviatoslav was born in the city of Kovel, Ukraine. At sixteen, he became interested in drawing. For fourteen years he continued his studies as an artist/ painter. He attended and graduated from the Odessa Art College and the National Academy of Painting in Kyiv. Sviatoslav, a member of the Union of Artists, has participated in exhibitions of the Union of Artists of Ukraine and his own personal events.

Sviatoslav credits his grandfather, Alexander Manelyuk, a graphic designer, as being his first teacher. His grandfather taught him to appreciate the beauty of nature, especially landscapes with their endless varieties.

Among other art projects, Sviatoslav is currently illustrating books. Lately, he has become interested in digital art with its endless possibilities.

Dear Reader,

If you enjoyed reading **TOM SHARP: THE MAN AND THE LEGEND (A Novel)** please help promote the book by posting a review on Amazon.com and following Charlie Steel on social media.

https://charliesteel.net/
https://www.facebook.com/charlie.steel.794
https://www.goodreads.com/author/show/3484434.Charlie_Steel
https://www.amazon.com/author/charliesteel

Charlie Steel can also be contacted at CharlieSteel.TaleWeaver.USA@gmail.com or by writing to the following address:

Charlie Steel
c/o Condor Publishing, Inc.
PO Box 39
Lincoln, Michigan 48742

Warm greetings from ***Condor Publishing, Inc.***

www.ingramcontent.com/pod-product-compliance
Lightning Source LLC
Chambersburg PA
CBHW020326030826
48979CB00020B/281

* 9 7 8 1 9 3 1 0 7 9 6 2 4 *